John Wright

The Sixth Work of Original Poems

John Wright

The Sixth Work of Original Poems

ISBN/EAN: 9783337401276

Printed in Europe, USA, Canada, Australia, Japan

Cover: Foto ©Andreas Hilbeck / pixelio.de

More available books at **www.hansebooks.com**

THE SIXTH WORK OF

ORIGINAL POEMS;

AND THE THIRD DESIGNATED

The Privilege of Man:

BY JOHN WRIGHT;

TOGETHER WITH

A SHORT SKETCH OF THE FAMILY,
AND LIFE OF THE AUTHOR;

BARD OF CLEVELAND,

MORAL PHILOSOPHER, AND UNIVERSAL PHILANTHROPIST;

AUTHOR OF THREE THOUSAND PAGES

COMPRISING EIGHT HUNDRED SUBJECTS,

RELIGIOUS, MORAL, AND PASTORAL.

LONDON:
PUBLISHED BY WILLIAM CHARLTON,
417, OXFORD STREET.

PRICE FIVE SHILLINGS AND SIXPENCE.
MDCCCLX.

TO HER GRACIOUS MAJESTY

Queen Victoria,

THIS WORK,

(AS AN EVERLASTING MEMORIAL,)

Is most humbly and respectfully Dedicated,

BY THE AUTHOR.

PROEM.

THE Grand Sylvanic, Prophetic, and Poetic Car; is yet upon its wheels, with strong elastic springs of genius, in truth well set, and moves with more than telegraphic speed, to wend its way from Deity, to man, who has the privilege in time to speak, in audience with his Maker! A word of caution, in sublimity: with earnest true simplicity, decked in the garb of sweet humility; I freely give, to those alone, of whom it has been said, " a word is quite sufficient."

Vast stretch of mind we have, in this our day, if rightly used, would far surpass anterior nobs of ancient date, tho', thanks is due to them, from us, who reap the benefit of light, which shone, in darker ages of the world, nor yet can be removed; the spark then kindled, now hath brighten'd into flame, and may through vigilance, illustrious shine! not as stars in dimness; but as suns immortal! in the blaze of Gospel day! While in the garden we are sat; can view the bud, the blossom, and the rose, with lovely odoriferous fume, expand, and well diffuse its sweet, delicious, and life giving breath! then look upon the fruitful trees, by proper culture brought to yield the best of fruit, for man to cull, and thus regale himself amid the chequer'd, changing scenes of human life, as vast mutations here, (in time,) have good effect, when rightly used, " The Privilege of Man."

In time, and while eternal ages roll, may yet progress; while soaring, thus may reach the highest pinnacle of fame, on earth, embodied all within, through faith in Christ alone, wherein, is famous dignity possess'd, (but not of meritorious right, by man acquir'd,) and then, beyond the bounds of time and space, transplanted, where the noblest pitch of honour shall be given, 'mid all the worthies bright, in every age, to soar in high extatic joy, increasing more and more, as endless ages roll, tho' perfect in its own degree, yet never reach the extremity!—Enjoyment is, " The Privilege of Man!"

Thus, man, with faculties of body and of mind, alive ; and all
eclat with spirit of harmonic song, embued ; and every string in
perfect tune, when each shall sound in sweetest strains, " the love
of God to man !"   Where nobler scenes shall be display'd, than
men or angels ever saw, nor yet the highest dignity conceive,
bright as the prospect is, yet brighter far remains to be explor'd,
when Christ himself the bright and Morning Star : with twice
ten thousand satellites around his throne shall stand, in robes of
righteousness to shine as He shall then appear, more brilliant than
the sun ! in splendid beauty and enjoyment ; world without end !
Amen.

But, what the burden of the flesh, within the vale, deprives
man of ; when the cumbrous mass dissolves, to mix and decom-
pose the well constructed frame wherein the soul of man in time
exists, then from the highest pinnacle of Zion's hill, shall man
behold his Maker, God, and King, in Jesu's lovely face, to shine
in all magnificence and glory, equal with Himself to be through
one eternal day.   This is the Privilege of Man ! but could I speak
with Gabriel's tongue, or write with Photographic art, the lines
with golden pen dipped in the precious crimson blood of Jesus
Christ, the lovely Lamb, for sinners slain, altho' the word be
truth itself, indelible and sure, the picture too, a true resemblance
of that lovely face, whose smile brought peace on earth, some
hardly could believe, the Privilege of Man ! 'Tis such, as angels
and archangels, in their blest abode, desired to see, tho' not per-
mitted.   But there to see and know, and well explore the golden
mines of rich crystallic gems so bright and dignified 'mid all the
splendours of yon city fair, superb, and healthy, where sweet
zephyrs waft their balmy breeze, of grand salubrious air ; and
every breath is vital ! Mark ! none but those who're pure, and
free from every stain or spot, to mar the splendid robe of righteousness in which they each are clad.   See now, the prospect, and
behold (with eyes prepared for beatific sight ;) Jesus, the lovely
King of kings : in glory sit ! Thus contemplate the high delight
in which you there participate with body and with mind, all equal
in perfection with Himself ! Mark ! 'tis no penumbram ; nor yet
presumption for my pen to write, or me to state, as Christ himself
declares it shall be so ! Rejoice my fellow man, rejoice with me,
amid the gloom of earthly things, again I say rejoice ! in time and
then eternity shall welcome thee to sing the sweet poetic song of
Moses and the Lamb in nobler strains above ! with all thy friends,
" The Privilege of Man !"

GREAT AYTON, 1860.

MEMOIR OF THE AUTHOR.

'Tis with great reluctance I now take up the pen to write of self, and more to gratify the curiosity of others than to suit my own inclination, for that would be to leave it alone altogether, nevertheless as I write for the benefit of others, I must in accordance with their request, give at least a short epitome of my life. Guisbro' is my birthplace, and is situate in the centre of the beautiful vale of Cleveland, hence the origin of my title (viz.,) " The Bard of Cleveland."

I have known personally four generations of our family. My Grandfather, (Richard Wright,) was a labouring man, and wrought 50 years on the Lowther's Estate, (Wilton Castle,) in Cleveland; at present the seat of Sir John Lowther, Bart. Ann, or Nanny, as Grandmother was called, kept a little shop, and sold groceries, with other small things, by which, with economy and grace, she was enabled to bring up a large family. My Father, (John Wright,) was the youngest of ten, five of which died in infancy, and the other five, (three sons and two daughters,) lived to a patriarchal age. I was well acquainted with them all, and with their varied progenies, and to their credit be it spoken, (not with egotistic pomp,) they were strictly moral, as far as I know, though I am aware Morality is not Christianity ; yet it is a natural source, of which spring I am speaking, and we are accountable to God for our actions, not our Christianity, else we

should be all on the back ground. Grace is a gift, virtue is ac-
quired. Among them was not found a drunkard, a swearer, or a
sceptic, nor did I know any of them rich, or any poor : they were
of the inventive faculty, making their own way by honest industry ; with high emotions this I speak, and gratitude to God, for
grace and abilities thus given. My Father, to business was a son
of Crispin, brought up, or trained to form good understandings.
I use this term, because it comprises everything that he made for
the exterior of the foot. Witness the patent obtained a few years
ago by him and my Brother, R. Wright, of Richmond in Yorkshire, for a very valuable improvement in boots and shoes, which
continues in operation by the surviving patentee, (who was once
Foreman for Mr. Hobey, corner of St. James Street, London.)
They appear to have been, and still continue, a family of noble in-
dependent spirit, not mean, low, and crouching, submitting to
wrongs for the sake of favour ; but the reverse, from principle,
must, and will speak the truth, with, or against them, being taught
this by their Grandfather, whom I believe was a christian, always
maintaining family devotion. His advice to us when on a visit,
was, " Mind and be honest my lads, and speak truth, then you
can look anybody in the face." By acting thus, through faith in
Christ ; have been kept from gross enormities, and as I believe
from want, and more, with every needful thing endowed.

> " We want but little here below,
> Nor want that little long."

My Father having learnt his business at Coatham, went to
London for improvement in 1802, was with Mr. Mc'Lauran, of
London Wall, and Mr. Gibbs of Ludgate Hill, two years ; and
was a member of the Wesleyan Society, the Rev. J. Benson was
his Class Leader. From London he returned home, and commenced business at Guisbrough ; then married Nancy Hutton, of
Newton, of humble industrious family. In the year 1807, Feb.
17th, I was born ; and my Parents when I was a year old, removed to Stokesley, where they brought up a family of eight
children, (on the birth of the last my Mother died,) and but four
of them now remain. Richard (my only surviving, and eldest

Brother,) resides at Richmond, where he has been 30 years in business; and my two Sisters, Hannah, and Mary, who having had good educations, and also learnt the several businesses of Boot Binding, Dress and Bonnet Making, together with Poonah Painting and other Fancy Work, determined with heroic spirit, to make their own way in the world; so at an early age, they left their Father's house, and crossed the Atlantic Ocean, where they got married, and are now living in peace and comfort, with their families, in the United States of America. My Father then, soon made an independency, and went to his Daughters, with whom he stayed awhile; and then went to Virginia, where he commenced and carried on for two years the Tanning and Currying, or Leather business. Not finding that to answer his purpose, as they truck, or barter, with little or no money; he brought his stock to Baltimore, sold off, returned to England, and invested his capital in the Patent of which I spoke; and at 60 years of age, re-commenced his old business, at Stokesley, where amongst his friends, he soon procured a second independency; and again at his daughters' request returned to America, where he finished his course, at the age of 77 years, March 3rd, 1857, at the house of his Daughter, Mrs. Mary Siver, Bridgeport, Connecticut.

At my own request I was taken from school, at the age of ten years, and commenced the Shoemaking business, with Father, and Brothers: (I of course wanted to be a man along with the rest.) Ten years I was at home with them, attentive to business, which did not agree with me, for I was the subject of Epilepsy, from the age of seven years, and have been ever since, to the present day; and with David I can say in truth "it was good for me that I was afflicted." In my twentieth year my Father engaged me to Mr. E. Dent of Stokesley, to learn the Hair-dressing business in six weeks, which I did, and then went to Mr. W. Booth in Stockton, one month, for improvement; it was then near May-Day. Father went with me to Guisbro', and took a single room, or Shop for me, of E. Pulman, where I commenced business: Father furnished me with a few combs, and perfumery, combing blocks, hair, &c., and gave me 10s. to start with as a fortune, and I thought it was very good and kind of him so to do. Thus situate, I was quite happy, tho', for several months made not more than

MEMOIR OF THE AUTHOR.

from 2s. 9d. to 3s. 6d. per week. Having plenty of leisure, I now commenced my studies, by reading Mason's Essay on Self-Knowledge, and other good books. As I had been brought up to the Church, and Wesleyan principles of Religion, was thus prepared, through grace, to follow the Christian faith : and in the same year, composed my first Poem, by a wonderful impulse, which when I had wrote quite astonished me, You will find it in my first work, page 100.

In the year 1828, I married Elizabeth Boyes, of Guisbro', of whom my Father approved, as (to use his own expression,) " she was a chip off a good block." Her Grandfather, W. Boyes, was a farmer at Barnaby, near Guisbro', 50 years, on the Chaloner's Estate : he was a strict churchman, and lived to a good old age. Her Father, W. Boyes, lived at Guisbro', and assisted the old man at Barnaby, he was a member of the Wesleyan Society 60 years. Their several ages were 95 and 85 years.

For twenty one years I attended my business, and wrote at leisure, for my own pleasure and mental improvement. I was then induced by Mr. John Havelock (relation to General Havelock,) to publish, but I had not means to do it; for the little money my wife and I had by the old principal got together, was fastened up in some premises which I had bought, and none of my friends would prove their friendship to me in that time of need. But convinced it was my duty to publish the work I had written for the weal of mankind, I determined to sell my property, throw my money into the concern, give up my business, and devote myself entirely to study. This I did, at a sacrifice of £500, which I joyfully threw into the lap of Providence, by whose direction I have thus far moved, 14 years; during five summers of which, my wife and I travelled with a little pony and gig, to sell the books. Since that I have gone off to the varied counties of England, to sell my consecutive works, and receive orders for fresh ones.

My children were five, three sons and two daughters : two sons died in infancy, my second son, William, born in the year 1830, I brought up to the hair-dressing business; and when I gave it up, I sent him to York for improvement, and he has never since been with, us except on a visit for a few months occasionally, when he came home for study. I had given him a good education, and he had a natural thirst for knowledge, to satisfy which he travelled in various parts of the world, and learned several languages. At the present time, he is exploring the far West, of America. My Daughter Jane Ann, (born 1835,) has been afflicted with St. Vitus's Dance, from the age of six months, which malady still continues. My Daughter Elizabeth (born 1838,) is an extraordinary intellectual girl, who at the age of nine years, read the Golden Treasury, likewise the Bible through, in one year; from which time has been progressing, as will be seen by a prospectus, (at the end of this book,) of a work she intends publishing.

My first publication was designated Anacreontic Poems, in which is contained an Epic Poem, (The History of Joseph and his Brethren,) also The Wonderful Pyramidical Figure of Jacob's Ladder, reading from top to bottom, and from bottom to top, to the same purport: 2000 copies of this work were printed in 1847.

1000 copies of my second (A Gem for Every One,) was printed in 1849.

1000 of my third (Comfort, Man was never made to Mourn,) was printed in 1852.

1200 of my fourth (The Privilege of Man,) was printed in 1854. And 1200 of the fifth, (the second on the Privilege of Man,) in 1857. The whole of these works contain 240 pages each.

This is the sixth work, and third on the Privilege of Man; in which I give 12 pages more, for the insertion of this extract, with a new and correct Lithographic Portrait of the Author.

The seventh work is now in a progressive state.

It may be thought I have had some special friend, to assist in the publication of these several works; but no, though publishing originalities is a very expensive thing, (which is only known to authors,) and mine have cost me not less than £2000, yet I never had the value of one penny but what I have laboured for day and night alternately, and burnt the midnight oil. I am struck with wonder and amazement, (when I think,) to know from whence the money came, as nothing was I born with, nothing had I left by others, and this I humbly state, nothing in debt, except a debt of gratitude to Him, from whence all blessings flow. This, this I can never pay, but Jesus doth forgive! thanks to His lovely

B

holy name, through whom I trust a legacy to leave, to benefit mankind, in after years, as well as at the present. The golden screw of providence is turned by His own hand; nor can it ever fail: the threads of which, are made so fine, that nature, art, nor wit, can ever see, to break! and yet are made so strong, that all the powers of earth, and hell, could ne'er destroy. "The weak, or foolish things of this world, are made to confound the wisdom of the wise." Still it may be asked, "where did you get your money, all this to pay, and keep your family besides?" 'Tis all a mystery to me, as well as you, and ever shall, excepting this, we have to live by faith and works united. Tho' at forty years of age I might have lived a little, idle, independant man with £30 per year; but (as I stated heretofore,) my little all I cast into the lap of Providence, and thus I move from day to day, nor ever wanted bread, and trust I never shall. The statement which our Saviour made I fully do believe, "Man shall not live by bread alone, but by every word that proceedeth out of his mouth."

Thus, have my time and talents been spent I trust, in the service of Him who gave them, though with many imperfections, and at the best, nothing whereof to boast. Sensible of my responsibility, I still move on; altho' my locks are white with age, and body feeble grown, the mind still soars to things sublime, and feeds upon the sweetest mental food, enjoying lasting pleasures, which the world can neither give nor take away. A little time will finish my career on earth, and then the great grand secret will be known, and all my labors left behind, to follow in succession. Though no reward on earth I claim, yet blessings I receive from Him, (the God of Love,) who judges right, and acts the same; to whose kind care I now commit myself, with no sad doubt or fear, but in sweet lively faith, to Jesus Christ my all resign; and on the civil list of Providence depend, for that assistance which my former works require to benefit mankind.

My life is now ended. and yet I'm alive,
To look reminiscences o'er:
Base envy and rancour, at this may connive;
If so, I shall give them some more!

The Privilege of Man.

THE UNIVERSAL CONCERT.

I CANNOT sing a gloomy ditty,
   Or write a jarring verse ;
I must be harping something pretty,
   And pleasing to rehearse,
In nature's lovely book, I read
   Good lessons, not a few ;
To which, all men of mind take heed,
   And own her subjects true.
Retaining in the memory, things
   Of sweet and lovely cast ;
Repudiating all that brings
   Discord, from first to last.
Our time is short, yet, life is sweet,
   If we but exercise

Ourselves, in order to repeat
   The song, of all the wise.
How many pleasing themes, present
   Themselves unto our view!
Inciting joy, and true content,
   Obtain'd by over few.
Where'er I take my walk, or stand
   To contemplate the scene;
A charming vision is at hand,
   Splendid, as nature's Queen!
Forth in the pleasing spring, when all
   Harmonious birds rejoice!
I hear the little songsters call,
   " Man! tune thy noble voice.
Strike up the note, and join the choir,
   Along with us who fly!
And touch the sweet poetic lyre,
   To raise your music high.
You can with heart, and tongue put forth,
   The grand harmonic sound:
Which brings bright heaven, down to earth,
   Where Paradise is found!"
The sentiment, methinks I feel,
   And hear in every breeze:
The morning, or the vesper peal,
   High jostling in the trees.
While Sol's reviving beams display,
   With energetic power,
The virtue of a charming day,
   In every plant, and flower.
Whence odorif'rous fumes arise,
   Delicious, sweet and grand:

Here, man has got a splendid prize,
　　When love, joins hand in hand.
But mark, the humming bees are throng,
　　Collecting every sweet ;
And while at work, they sing the song
　　In quota, all complete !
Then when the genial shower descends,
　　Upon the verdant fields ;
With native soil its virtue blends,
　　And fruit abundant yields,
For man, and beast ; yea, fish and bird ;
　　With every mortal thing ;
And then, the princely voice is heard,
　　In grateful strains to sing ;
High praises, to the God of heaven !
　　Munificent, and good :
For he, unmerited hath given,
　　To every thing its food.
Yea! more, far more than tongue can tell:
　　Is granted unto man !
And he, who feels it, knows it well ;
　　By Christ's atoning plan.
Ah ! this is harmony complete !
　　When saints and angels join.
To sing the song with love replete,
　　Where Jesus, starts the tune !
The grandest concert ever given,
　　(Till then) since time began ;
Commences at the gate of heaven !
　　To which, Christ welcomes man.
Where all unite to praise the Lord,
　　With golden harps well strung ;

2 B

Ten thousand, thousand in accord,
　　Join heart, and voice, and tongue.
The King of Kings! in grand display:
　　Jesus! we then shall see,
On that sweet Coronation Day,
　　To last, eternally!

CAUTION.

Ah! friends, and would you all be there?
　　Come now, within the gate;
And enter thus, by faith and prayer:
　　Or else, you'll be too late!

THE FALL AND RISE OF NATIONS!
JUDGMENT AND MERCY.

Hark! a voice from on high, 'tis the roar of a King;
　　Tremendous enough with the sword:
Destruction, on all the vile rebels to bring;
　　Pronounc'd by the word of the Lord!
" Because they would none of them hearken to me,
　　Nor come at the merciful call:
So now they must die, like an old rotten tree;
　　And Babel, shall surely fall!
While the nations around, to the ends of the earth,
　　Do witness the dreadful affair:
Sheer vengeance, with just indignation and wrath,
　　Shall hurry them off, in despair!

The whirlwind and tempest, will drive them away,
    Who are nought in the world but a pest :
Shall drink the base cup, to the dregs, in their day ;
    And I'll burn up their filthy old nest.
In their wickedness all shall be driven below ;
    Where drunkards, shall drink of the wine,
Mix'd up in the cell of perdition and woe,
    By the hand of justice divine !
Say, thus said the Lord God of Israel, drink ye ;*
    And be drunken, and spue, yea, and fall :
No more to arise, with the living to be,
    A madman, a pest, and a brawl !"
What an awful condition is this to mankind ?
    Given up by the God of all grace :
To hardness of heart, and a reprobate mind,
    His image, at once to erase.
A scourge, is base drinking ; the sword, is another ;
    Ordain'd by the powers of heaven :
The wine for yourself, and the sword for your brother !
    But shall they be taken, or given ?
We've used them too often, again and again ;
    Jerusalem couldn't be worse :
In the practice of which, tens of thousands are slain :
    And this, is to Britain, a curse !
But, the hand of the Lord, is stretch'd out to us yet,
    With the blessing of Jesus, for all !
Our sun is still shining, tho' soon it will set ;
    And we, to destruction may fall !
While the light of the Gospel, is held in our hand,
    Let us work by its principle, love :

* Jeremiah xxv. 27.

And drive the vile monster away from the land ;
  Or the candle of grace, shall remove.
'Tis the word of the Lord, I must use it again ;
  To remind you of what he declares :
The wicked are turned into hell, to remain ;
  But the righteous, in judgment, he spares.
Now, now is the time, or for ever too late !
  Don't weary the Lord, by delay :
Nor ask the great King, any longer to wait,
  But, turn from your evils, to-day.

This Poem was suggested on hearing a person say (while in a state of intoxication,) ostentatiously ! " I am just fulfilling scripture, by the practice of drinking ;" then he quoted a passage in the Bible,* (as the Devil can,) his purpose to maintain. I induced him to stay, till I found, and read to the company in the place, the whole chapter ; commenting on the same as follows :—"Drunkenness, and the sword, are two of the chief instruments used by the Almighty, for the destruction of the incorrigible ; and woe unto them, who fall victims to the same.

AN ADDRESS TO CONTEMPT.

AWTHORNE may write of poets, poor ;
  Who build their castles high,
In elements without a floor ;
  And have to beg, or die.

* Jeremiah xxv. 27.

I have no doubt but what he states,
　Is far too often true ;
Yet, some may ope the pearly gates,
　Of heav'nly bliss for you.
Who build your castles on the ground,
　And think them very strong ;
Yet by and bye, they'll not be found,
　To whom they now belong.
Celestial things are all unseen,
　Tho' felt by saints on earth ;
Who know the truth of what I mean,
　And realize its worth.
Terrestial things, are just for time ;
　And nothing more for sure :
But mind, (in sweet poetic rhyme,)
　For ever shall endure !
Then, let the poet sing his song,
　With profit and delight ;
If what he says, you can't find wrong,
　Surely it must be right.

MORAL.

Sweet words retort, in echo sweet !
　A smile induces such :
Whose language, you may soon repeat,
　And happen smile as much.

THE ROYAL MARRIAGE CANTATA.

THE Prince, and the Princess are one,
    In unity sweetly combin'd ;
And the Queen, has got a new son,
    Whom Providence now hath assign'd.
The rose, and the lily shall blow,
    In lustre, to flourish awhile ;
Where honour, and dignity grow,
    To merit Victoria's smile !
But that of their Father above,
    On the two united in one ;
(The spark of His heavenly love)
    Will shine, when the mortal has done !
Illustrious, and splendid on high :
    Tho' the flame be ignited below,
'Twill outshine the sun in the sky,
    And onward eternally go !
A wonderful creature is man !
    But what must the Deity be !
Who made, and ordained the plan,
    By which, the two sexes agree.
The banns, were first publish'd in heaven ;
    The knot, is securely tied :
And each, to each other is given,
    A partner, in love to abide.
May God bless the young " Royal pair :"
    And grant them, the smile of His face,
Whose guidance, protection, and care,
    Are jewels, preserved in grace.

Let health, and longevity here,
  With blessings of higher degree ;
The hearts of their family cheer,
  Wherever their station may be.
And then, when probation doth cease,
  In the valley of vision below ;
May each have a lasting increase
  Of favour, the King shall bestow !
On all, who His marriage attend !
  With garments, unspotted by sin :
Obtain'd at the hand of their Friend,
  Who bid them at once enter in.
To the joy of the " Bride and the Lamb !"
  And feast, on the heavenly store :
Prepar'd, by the noble I AM !
  Whose bounty is free, evermore.
The feast of the marriage above,
  Commenc'd in the casket below ;
Shines forth in the heart of true love,
  Which only recipients know.
Mankind, for this cause, are to leave*
  Their parents, in love to unite ;
Where truth, cannot virtue deceive :
  And right, answers duly to right !

* Ephesians v. 31.

MILK AND HONEY.

(TUNE "TOM AND JERRY.")

COME and taste along with me,
      Milk and honey.
Growing on the Gospel tree,
      Milk and honey.
Fountain head of liberty,
      Milk and honey.
Yes, I'll come and sip with thee,
      Milk and honey free.

Grapes are on the living vine.
      Ripe and ready.
Clusters growing plump and fine,
      Ripe and ready.
Jesus says they're yours and mine,
      Ripe and ready.
All their virtue is divine!
      Ripe and ready now.

Come and feast along with me,
      In fair Canaan.
Every splendour you shall see,
      In fair Canaan.
Blended with sweet harmony:
      In fair Canaan.
Lasting as eternity
      In the Promis'd Land!

THE RETORT TO BURNS' "MAN WAS MADE TO MOURN."

Poor Burns, a natural Poet he,
   (As many a judge hath said ;)
But now the work devolves on me,
   With my poor simple head.
May grace conduct my heart and pen,
   Base errors to detect ;
And publish to the sons of men,
   What God will not reject.
On that great day, when we appear
   Before the Judge of all,
Who gave the witty, charming ear,
   And loud prophetic call!
The power of prophecy's a gift,
   Which natural Poets have ;
Nor can it be obtain'd by thrift,
   Of any fool or knave.
So far from which was Robie Burn,
   Who took a partial view ;
And tells us, " Man was made to mourn."
   Tho' understood by few.
Methinks a foolish lesson we
   May wipe from out the book ;
Where simpletonians yet may be
   Oft meand'ring in the nook.
A dense black cloud hung o'er the head
   Of one whose day is past,

c

By comic metre often led,
　To puff a bitter blast.
The mourning subject he entails
　On all the human race ;
Who with him sorrily bewails
　Mankind, in such a case.
And while he turns the magic-reel,
　(Wounding the nobly free,)
Claps on a plaster, thus to heal
　The subject, few can see.
" But, let not this too much, my son,
　Disturb thy ambler cast ;
The work which I have boldly done,
　Is surely not the last.
A partial view of human kind,
　You here perceive I've given ;
But one is on the march you'll find,
　Which points the way to heaven.
The poor, oppressed, honest man,
　Surely had not been born,
But for God's pre-ordained plan,
　To comfort those that mourn."
" The death of sin and sorrow here,
　Brings life, and joy, and peace ;
To all, who by the compass steer,
　Till mortal life shall cease.
True faith in Christ, the prospect gives,
　Which opens out the store ;
And every one who in him lives,
　Shall live for evermore."
This is the bright side you perceive,
　Which Burns prognosticated ;

Should soon appear, and thus relieve
  The mind of what he hated.
Look through this telescope and see,
  The morning star appears!
Which shone from all eternity,
  And shall to endless years.
The first, the last, the only wise!
  Omnipotent, divine!
Mark! all who strive shall with him rise,
  And in his image shine!
As sons immortal, bright, and fair,
  No mourning aspect then,
Shall intervene, mid sapient air,
  In every breath, Amen!

BLESSED STATE OF THE RIGHTEOUS.

OH! how blest is the man that feareth the Lord,
  And all his commands doth obey!
The full power he receives to feed on his word,
  And drink of the brook by the way!
To His name will he give the thanks of his heart,
  For peace and contentment within;
The pathway of holiness gave him the start,
  And led to the conquest of sin.
Nor is he afraid at the tidings of ill,
  Whose heart is thus stedfast and sure;
Believing the Lord will his promise fulfil,
  While the Sun and the Moon shall endure.

His soul is establish'd in grace while he lives,
  Nor when he departs will he' shrink
From the faith he receives of Jesus, who gives
  A portion in every link
Of the chain of Providence, reaching to heaven;
  Tho' bound to the earth with a tie
Which must (in conclusion,) asunder be riven,
  And yet it shall mount up on high !
Whatever the wounds be, inflicted in time,
  Mortality buries the whole;
Th' immortal then soars to a heavenly clime,
  No more being subject to fall !—
Tho' none can unravel the mystery, known
  Alone where the secret's reveal'd,
In the bliss of the Lord, (reserv'd for his own,)
  Th' mysterious book is unseal'd !
Th' ungodly shall see it, and gnash with his teeth,
  For ever consumed by his lust;
Who never can rise from his cavern beneath,
  The God of all mercy is just.

GOOD COUNSEL FROM AN OLD FRIEND.

WHEN bleak December's surly blast
    Strips naked all the trees,
Which lately bore the amber cast,
    In the autumnal breeze.

True emblem of the man I saw,
　So weary and infirm ;
Whose body feels the winds that blow,
　And every rising storm.
While furrowed cheeks bespeak his years,
　And silvery locks foretell
Mortality in part appears
　To ask if all is well !—
He took me gently by the hand.
　Smiling, said thus to me ;
" I'm bound to Canaan's happy land,
　Beyond the swelling sea !—
Just step a pace or two and wend
　'Longside an aged sire ;
For shortly all my days will end,
　And I shall soon retire.
Altho' in youth, when things were gay,
　Or manhood's noble strength ;
Me seldom thought 'twould pass away,
　Nor time ere spin its length.
Full three score years and ten I've seen,
　My glass is nearly run ;
While numerous objects pass between
　The rise and setting sun ;
Yet, let not this disturb thee, child,
　Or tease thy tender breast ;
Tho' youthful passions oft run wild,
　And seldom are at rest.
By inexperience, pomp, and pride,
　Young people go astray ;
Without a friend their steps to guide,
　Or point the safest way.
c 2

But listen to my counsel, dear,
  And something you may leain,
In after life your heart to cheer,
  Where otherwise you'd mourn.
Never be lavish of your time,
  Be parsimonious here;
While every season rings 'a chime,
  Which you may buy too dear.
Thus, like " Ben Franklin's whistle," which
  He bought when but a boy;
Paid all his money to be rich,
  And got a simple toy.
'Twas fancy, whim, and self conceit,
  (As afterwards he knew,)
That urged him to this costly treat,
  For which he had to rue.
But sage experience proves to me,
  The vanity of things,
In this wide sublunary sea,
  Nor lasting comfort brings.
And now, young man, my time is short,
  I must no longer stay,
If you have but one lesson caught,
  Live well in youth of day!
A few more yeais and you may be
  As old as I am now;
And then you'll happen think of me,
  When back begins to bow.
But one thing mark, and dont forget,
  That time flies on apace,
Wherein a portion we have set,
  To find in heav'n a place.

So when this mortal life shall end,
  · To all eternity ;
You there enjoy a better friend
  Than e'er you found in me."

———

"THE RIGHTS OF MAN," VIE. PRIVILEGE.

THE Rights of Man, in reason bound,
  Of which " Tom Paine " could boast,
Without one spot of solid ground,
  Whereon to march his Host.
But man, with privilege, has more
  Of what belongs to mind,
Than reason ever could explore,
  Or earthly wisdom find.
Yet, such will lift their puny arm
  To strike Omnipotence ;
Tho' tott'ring, faint, within the qualm,
  And feel its virulence.
But I should say, the Rights of Man,
  (Had he alone his due,)
Would fix the base contemptuous ban,
  With privileges few.
Yet, grace extends beyond his right,
  Immeasurably free ;
Nor can it be obtain'd by might,
  Or won by land or sea.
The gift of God to man is such
  As he could never buy,

Altho' he bears the stamp, or touch,
  Of Deity on high!
Mark, this is privilege indeed!
  Which "right" could not obtain;
That will both soul and body feed,
  And life eternal gain.
We had no right to disobey!
  When that was done, what then?
The penalty was due, to pay!
  And re-instate us men.
You now perceive 'tis mercy all,
  Immense, and unconfin'd,
Which rais'd man high above the fall,
  With dignity of mind!

PREVENTION IS BETTER THAN CURE.

WHILE youth are in health and vigour of life,
  Whose passions are active and free,
The lessons of truth or falsehood are rife,
  And bend like the soft willow-tree.

Necessity lays on their parents' so wise,
  To see that they're trained aright,
While watching the progress of such, in the rise,
  To tutor and polish them bright.

Otherwise they will grow unwieldly and coarse,
  Self-will'd as the wild asses colt,

For nature moves on, nor driven by force,
  Propelling the limp or the halt.

Oft blame is attach'd to the young, where 'tis not,
  While the aged incline to go free,
But mark who have fixed the stain or the blot,
  Just open your eyes now and see.

Behold the contempt, with indignity shown,
  To the indigent parent at home ;
Who, ashamed of his state, nor have it be known,
  He'd up with his staff for to roam.

In pursuit of some bread the mendicant moves,
  With him 'tis back end of the week,
His fingers are cold, for he hasn't got gloves,
  So petty for beggars to seek.

Methinks I can see the old man on his way,
  He looks up, and knocks at the door,
Then with a sham'd face, in the eve of the day,
  He mutters, " Remember the Poor."

Now think of the subject, tho' I've cut it short,
  And weigh all the matter for sure,
Nor ever make light of the thing you have bought,
  Prevention is better than cure.

REJOICE EVERMORE !

Rejoice in the Lord for ever, and more
    Delighted with praise thou shalt be;
In realization of that blessed store,
    Reserved in heaven for thee !
Rejoice evermore, (with the saints upon earth,)
    For ever and more did I say ?
Yes, testing the truths of immaculate worth,
    Rejoicing for ever and aye !
"Saint Paul, and Isaiah," recommended the plan
    To the church, (in primitive days,)
As highly befitting the station of man,
    To live in the action of praise.
Rejoice evermore, we have cause for the same,
    In honor of Christ who was slain !
Then sing hallelujahs to his blessed name,
    Rejoice, and repeat it again.
In extatic joy, (with emotion of fire,)
    The spark to a flame shall arise ;
When kindled by love, with an ardent desire,
    To obtain the seat of the wise.
The angels in heaven rejoice at the sight,
    When man is made happy on earth,
The reciprocity enhances delight,
    When he has obtain'd the new birth.
Rejoice in the casket, now ever and more,
    While it is the seat of the soul ;
And then your rejoicings will never be o'er,
    While ages eternal shall roll !

SINCERITY.

My dearest Emma, I incline,
  By love's most ardent flame,
In principle to call thee mine,
  And we be one in name.
The truth I state, without a joke
  Or vague duplicity ;
Let's tie the knot (which can't be broke,)
  In bonds of unity.
My heart with thine I trust is one
  In recripro' respond,
And let me know the work is done,
  By such as won't abscond.
Altho' the principle of love
  Is seated in the heart,
Methinks the same will not remove,
  Or ever hence depart.
Could I in its embrace recline
  With those emotions blest,
" Dear Emma" should be always mine,
  In peace and heavenly rest.
By faith in Christ I hope to live,
  And work his will with pleasure ;
My hand in this I freely give
  To thee, my earthly treasure.

Composed at Manchester, July 10th, 1854, expressly for Sam.

AN ANSWER TO A LETTER

From Mr. John Campbell, (a Friend,) composed on si gh
in 15 minutes, March 7th, 1855.

IERCE winds may blow, keen frosts may pinch,
   And tempests whirl thee round ;
I hope thou'll never dare to flinch,
   With head above the ground.
For, if thou keep the hoisted sail,
   (The banner of true love,)
The storms of life can not prevail,
   Thy standard to remove !
Altho' we here on earth may part,
   Again old friends shall meet,
(Especially while one in heart,)
   And each, each other greet.
Our social intercourse on earth,
   Wherein we've often met,
To tacit language will give birth,
   Nor is it ended yet.
But when sweet Jesus speaks within,
   We hear the still small voice
Proclaiming peace, (here ends the din,)
   Which used to be our choice.
Now, now our converse is sublime—
   With sentiment divine !
Tho' pilgrims while we're thus in time,
   Our graces here must shine.—
That when we see the glory of
   Each other, with our King !

In transports of redeeming love,
   Shall loud hosannas sing !—
Farewell, my "friend," I'll meet thee there,
   Or happen shortly here ;
By faith, remember me in prayer,
   With neither doubt nor fear.
To Christ alone all praise is due,
   For every blessing given ;
In time we've realized a few,
   The major part's in heaven—
Where storms and tempests are no more,
   Nor clanking wars annoy ;
Our peaceful souls, on Canaan's shore,
   Till then, my friend, good bye.

THE STAFF AND BEAUTY OF AGE.

WHEN man hath reach'd meridian day,
   The evening shades unfold ;
His former life has pass'd away,
   Just like a tale that's told.

And when the gloomy night draws on,
   His sun is well nigh set ;
He now reflects on what he's done,
   And half begins to fret.

But, let the vain desponding thought,
   Into oblivion drop ;

D

Or else by it he's surely caught,
  And sinks without a prop.

Jesus, the staff of hoary age,
  Supports the drooping frame,
Of those in life's concluding stage,
  Who hang upon his name.

By faith alone, which cannot fail,
  The man who keeps his hold,
Although the tempest may prevail,
  It makes the hero bold.

Thus, launching out into the deep,
  Where billows foaming swell ;
He trusts the Lord his soul to keep,
  And land, " where all is well."

While on the verge of Jordan here,
  By faith in Christ we stand ;
And view fair Canaan bright and clear,
  " The holy, happy land."

Where age and death no more, forsooth,
  Disturb our sweet repose ;
We flourish in immortal youth,
  As " Sharon's lovely rose ! "

THE ORIGIN OF DRESS.

Who pride themselves in foolish dress,
May happen come to great distress
  Before the same is worn :
Yet, pride at heart may lurk within,
Where dwells the origin of sin,
  In which mankind are born.

Tho' rags and tatters you may wear,
Or happen go half nak'd and bare,
  For want of needed pelf ;
Yet, 'neath a shabby coat may be
The thing that prompts your vanity,
  And pride will shew itself.

But, dignity can never find
In dress, whereon to feed the mind,
  Or gratify good sense ;
'Twas pride that first occasion'd dress,
To hide our shameful nakedness,
  And drove our virtue hence.

Who in habiliments are vain,
Just lose the thing they should obtain,
  And glory in their shame !
Jesus for sin did once atone ;
Humility, and that alone,
  Exalts to highest fame !

DECEPTIVE DRESS.

IGHT scrutiny of man to man,
　　Evinces much to be observ'd,
By those who oft contrary ran,
　　With strength enough to be unnerv'd.

The stock is taken of his dress,
　　Habiliments attract the eye,
Then judge him little, big, or less
　　Than whom the strangers apt to try.

And if the coat he wears be gay,
　　With all the rest to correspond,
What homage to the man we pay,
　　Nor readily from him abscond.

A courteous bow, " Dear Sir," with smile,
　　(Then loudly rings the parlour bell,)
" Step in, and take a seat awhile,
　　I hope yourself and family's well :

A glass of wine, sir, do partake,
　　A biscuit, too, I here present,
Pray take a little iced cake,
　　Perhaps you've come to pay your rent ? "

" Oh no, dear madam, no not I,
　　My errand's of another cast ;
I've come, your ladyship, to try
　　To get relief, for I am fast."—

" Hark ye ! good man, you must be wrong,
    Appearance half convinces me
That you to better class belong,
    Your statement don't with dress agree.

But if what you have said be true,
    Nothing have I to give, I'm sure ; "
All that was done, she seem'd to rue :
    And pointed him the way t' door.

" Ah, now," quoth he, " the fine and fair,
    Such kind and free reception meet ;
But poverty must not come there,
    Nor yet enjoy my lady's treat.

No wine, or biscuit would have been
    Presented to the mendicant,
Had his appearance shown him mean,
    Short answer he'd have got with taunt.

So much for his appearance, mark,
    It entertain'd the unwelcome guest ;
And kept the lady in the dark,
    Till he had tasted of her best.

MORAL.

If neatness and order, with etiquette, prove
    Deceptive to ignorant folk,
I'd have it be manifest, only in love,
    And smile at the wonderful joke.

TO MORROW!

WHEN doubts and fears your peace assail,
Striving o'er reason to prevail,
Then place them on laconic scale ;
        Say, " call again to-morrow."

And if the day present the same,
You know the visitors by name,
But don't incline to play their game,
        Say, " call again to-morrow."

The " Traitor" won't your plan admire,
He'll happen come with vengeful ire,
And strive to shove you in the fire
        To-day, before to-morrow.

Repudiate him with the shield
Of faith, which you must nobly wield,
And then, his destiny is seal'd :
        Nor shall he see to-morrow.

Mankind in time are sure to have
Temptations from the subtle " knave,"
Who ne'er perform'd an action brave,
        The cause of all our sorrow.

Without an invitation, will
With doubt and fear your bosom fill,
While hope and joy they strive to kill,
        To-day, before to-morrow.

Fair virtue's lovely smiling train,
You must in truth, to-day obtain,
And hold the same, if you would gain
    A safeguard for to-morrow.

I heard " Old Fear " say thus to " Doubt,"
" The villain now hath found us out,
He minds to-day what he's about :
    We have no chance to-morrow ! "

MORAL.

 Never defer until to-morrow,
  What should be done to-day ;
 Or you will find by grief and sorrow,
  The evil of delay.

THE TRAITOR'S CONFESSION.

I cannot say but he is right,
Who always has his armour bright,
And uses it with all his might;
His instruments he holds so tight,
And with dexterity polite,
We never need with him to fight;
Both morn, and noon, and all the night,
In faith and hope he takes delight,
Of him we cannot make a bite.
Thus, Doubt and Fear are put to flight,
No more obtrude upon our sight,
Where we can build to Zion's height,
    Eternity's to-morrow !

A WRONG CALCULATION PUT RIGHT.

HE misfortunes of mankind, do always appear
  To magnify much their amount,
A peep through the glass, far away to bring near,
  Will settle the awkward account.
They, Providence charge with the ills that befall
  Themselves, and their property too,
But never tax self with misconduct, at all,
  And this is the way that they do!
Or to suit their vile taste the public, say they,
  Bring all their calamities here ;
To spoil their best work in end of the day,
  And put them in tremorous fear.
Mark, "time and chance fall on the worthiest men,"
  (As Solomon truly hath said ;)
Tho' the foolish and wise may handle the pen,
  Yet wisdom's the honoured head.
The mopish, the peevish, and indolent, will
  Contrary to providence steer ;
'Tis not in his heart or his mind to be still,
  And wait till the daylight appear.
Then, then to behold the fair beauty of whom
  The wisdom of man couldn't find,
Till Jesus with dignity rose from the tomb,
  And gave him an excellent mind !
Superior to all the contingencies here,
  And proof against every foe ;
By faith, hope, and charity, never to fear,
  However the changes may go.

Nor tax we again the immaculate friend,
   Who alone can help us in need ;
Whose goodwill is ever, and world without end,
   T'wards us, both in word and in deed !

THE CROSS AND CROWN.

THE Christian may expect to meet
   With crosses on his way
To everlasting rest, the seat
   Of bliss in endless day!
The best example ever given
   For us to patronize,
Is that of Christ, who open'd heaven
   By royal sacrifice !
He bore the cross for us, and we
   The cross must bear for him ;
And then the crown eternally
   Is ours, likewise the gem.
Which glitters in meridian day,
   With light and love to shine ;
Nor can it fade or pass away ;
   The Cross and Crown be mine!

PAST, PRESENT, AND TO COME.

BEHOLD, what changes there have been,
  Since last we saw each other !
And what have we both felt and seen,
  My youths have lost their mother !
And I a lovely partner dear,
  Who always strove her best,
In every form my heart to cheer,
  And make me truly blest.
But, ah ! the scene has chang'd, and now
  The retrospective glance
Is all I do mantain to show,
  How happy I was once.
On which, so often ruminate
  With pleasure and with pain,
Although I cannot reinstate
  Myself, in bliss again.
Methinks I see my little flock,
  In pristine beauty smile !
With all simplicity unlock
  Each heart, to chat awhile ;
In reminiscence of the past,
  Alternately to speak ;
Nor ever dread the bitter blast
  Which now appears so bleak.
What we enjoy'd in former years,
  (Reality can prove,)
Hath left us all, in doubts and fears,
  And made a long remove.

That charming face, that brilliant eye,
  Which once attracted me ;
Are now no more—then tell me why
  They're gone eternally ?
All transient, fleeting joys on earth—
  (Each moment we perceive,)
Forbid to amplify our mirth ;
  And will at length bereave.
Who doting set their hearts upon
  Mankind, or minor things,
Will find, erelong, the whole are gone,
  Nor lasting comfort brings.
On "Christ" above, affections place,
  And let your heart be there ;
While often at the throne of grace
  You meet your friend in prayer !
Who thither hath gone up on high,
  Received gifts for men—
And will our every want supply,
  Until we meet again.
Where pain, and parting are no more—
  Whole families shall meet—
On Canaan's lovely, happy shore !
  And each, each other greet.
To know the why, and wherefore of
  Cross providences here,
Will much enhance the passion love,
  And every bosom cheer !
To see, that all things thus have wrought
  Together for our good—
Nor do we serve our God for naught,
  As Job, well understood.

Into whose hands I now would fall,
   There passive let me lay;
Until I hear my Saviour call,
   " Spring forth, and come away !"

IN MEMORY OF JAMES MONTGOMERY, ESQ. THE YORKSHIRE POET, SHEFFIELD.

Died April 30th, 1854, aged 82.

MONTGOMERY's vital spark has fled
   Beyond the bounds of time !
Though oft the Muses kindly led
   His mind, to songs sublime.
Parnassus' streams, therein did flow,
   When he was twelve years old ;
So ardent felt their genial glow,
   With sentiment untold.
The patriotic libertine,
   Nature, and truth combined ;
Throughout his life did him enshrine
   With dignity entwined.
The third of last September, I
   Receiv'd his autograph,
And saw the tear, fall from his eye,
   But now, he's dropp'd his staff ;
The conversation we had then,
   Was on both life and death ;
Said he, " Could I but live again,
   I'd well employ my breath."

My answer was, " I hope you have
   Thus far not liv'd in vain,
Though age may lure you to the grave,
   Nor care to live again.
Ah! no, friend Wright, I'm quite resign'd
   Unto my Maker's will,
Yet, more and more I feel inclin'd
   My duty to fulfill ;
Omissions of the same I do
   Sincerely now regret,
The day is spent, and evening too,
   My sun is nearly set.
I'm in my eighty-second year,
   And busy in the field,
Amid alternate hope and fear,
   Yet I am loath to yield.
Well, well, my venerable sire,
   You've nothing more to do,
But ask and have all you require,
   And thus enjoy it now.
This topic of discourse here clos'd,
   He then commenc'd another,
And said, to write you're still disposed,
   What is your subject, brother?
" ' The Privilege of Man,' in which
   Is centred all his treasure :"
Then said he, " I shall honor such,
   And patronize the measure.
God speed you well, I ne'er may live
   To see the work come out,
But here, my hand I freely give,
   'Twill prosper, there's no doubt.

E

I've read your " Comfort," and your " Gem,"
   By which I calculate
The spirit that is breath'd through them,
   In you will not abate.
" Go on," said he, " until we meet
   Where all our labours end,
And then the music shall be sweet,
   In presence of our Friend,*
Who tuned the string so sweet below,
   And caus'd the lyric move—
To Paradise we onward go,
   And join the Band above.
Where harmony throughout prevails,
   Loud hallelujahs swell—
And breezes waft in lovely gales,
   To sound the note, ' All's well ! ' "

ONE OF THE WORLD'S WONDERS!

WHAT a world of wonder is this !
   Tho' man is the object sublime;
And all from chaotic abyss,
   Sprang up in a moment of time.

The Sun, and the Moon, and the Stars
   Have each their locality given ;
And ride in their separate cars,
   Along the high vaulticle, heaven !

* Jesus Christ.

And yet with a flash of the mind,
   Direct to the origin, we,
By the teliscoparian, find
   The Author of all we can see.

And ah, for intelligent man !
   Whose knowledge and genius are such,
True wisdom hath formed the plan,
   Whereby the extremities touch.

A slight handed specimen, we
   Do obtain, while moving along
The wide clementary sea,
   To rectify all that is wrong.

Thus, thus to convey on a wire
   Good news to the nations around ;
Shot by the electric fire,
   Without the least vocalic sound !

'Tis now coming fast to a close ;
   But let the first message across
Be in the philanthrophic cause,
   And ride on the conquering horse !

Then praise to the donor be given,
   Who wrought out the wonderful plan ;
Similiation of earth unto heaven,
   By peace and good will unto man.

A MORAL STANDARD.

ACTIONS, when in the balance weigh'd,
　　Of justice, truth, and might;
Must have their bearing to decide,
　　In matters wrong or right.

And yet, no merit can we claim,
　　By word, or thought, or deed ;
'Tis all in virtue of His name,
　　Who did for sinners bleed.

And those who honor Him the most,
　　Are now and ever blest ;
With Father, Son, and Holy Ghost,
　　In righteousness are drest!

And such are God's peculiar choice,
　　Elect, and precious store ;
Who listen to their Saviour's voice,
　　And all His love adore !—

Mark, they who honor Him the most,
　　Will love, and serve Him best ;
Nor ever of their virtue boast,
　　Or speak of it in jest.

But modestly act well their part,
　　(In whatsoever sphere ;)
With true sincerity of heart,
　　Of moral evil clear.

A CURIOUS METHOD OF OBTAINING
KNOWLEDGE.

AR in the wilds of yonder west,
  Two witty jokers met;
Smoothly each other thus address'd,
  Expecting truth to get.
" Methinks (if I may make so bold,)
  I've seen you, sir, somewhere !"
The answer was, " the truth you've told,
  For I am always there."
This vague, and odd inquisito,
  Is used by Yorkshiremen;
As introductory to know
  Persons beyond their ken.
With whom would thus acquaintance claim,
  Strangers to each before;
Thinking the man will tell his name,
  And maybe something more.
But nay, the secret still is hid
  In wisdom's cunning head;
Retort was made to shut the lid,
  When he the needful said.
In full and short laconic style,
  Where Yorkshire couldn't press;
The Yankee turn'd about to smile,
  And left his friend to guess.

THE SMILE.

THE smile! pray what is that to me?
   I cannot smile at naught!
But when my soul is fill'd with glee,
   The sentiment is caught.

And others see the thing I feel,
   Within my bosom hid;
An honest smile can ne'er conceal
   The truth, beneath the lid.

An index to the mind, is found
   Upon the countenance,
Which gives a certain tone, or sound,
   By one expressive glance.

No living thing on earth can smile,
   Except the human race;
Nor was intended to beguile,
   But shew an honest face.

This privilege, (who search will find,)
   Is man's prerogative;
For he alone (that's blest with mind,)
   Can this expression give.

Then let it have its full design,
   Exemplifi'd by all;
Who wish in virtue's ways to shine,
   The great, as well as small.—

MORAL.

True simile, and image of
   His Author's placid face ;
The man whose principle is love,
   And smiles in Jesu's grace !

A QUERY, ONE HUNDRED YEARS TO COME!
THIS LIFE AND NEXT.

PART I.

PRAY who do you think will inhabit the earth,
   When those hereupon, shall have from it gone
     forth ;
               One hundred years to come ?
Mankind, who are jolly, and blithesome to-day,
Will then, as a shadow, have all pass'd away ;
               One hundred years to come !
Ten thousand to one, that a man shall remain,
On the face of the earth, his place to maintain,
               One hundred years to come !
Should the dear little baby in arms, be alive,
And ripen in time, the vast wreck to survive,
               One hundred years to come :
What a silly old man, the stripling would be !
With back bending, eyes dim, and the white almond
     tree ;
               One hundred years to come !
Yet he, with the passing, most certainly must

Return to his origin, " dust unto dust," *
     One hundred years to come !
The Beasts of the Forest, and Birds in the air,
Which frolic and gambol, to dust shall repair,
     One hundred years to come !
All spring, as the flower, and perish the same :
But leave not a vestige, excepting the name,
     One hundred years to come !
A fresh generation of things shall appear ;
And seem to those then, as these to us here :
     One hundred years to come !
The bright Sun will shine on the world, as at present ;
The morning appear, and the evening as pleasant,
     One hundred years to come !
The plough-boy shall whistle the song of the maid ;
And both shall be glad, when our heads are low laid,
     One hundred years to come !
In vision prospective my heart can rejoice,
To see them eclat, and to hear their sweet voice,
     One hundred years to come !
Cheer up, jolly folk, make the best of your day ;
Though you, with ourselves, shall have all fled away ;
     One hundred years to come !
Mechanics, and Artizans, Poets and all,
(Who are popular now,) will be then very small ;
     One hundred years to come !
But before I have done, you shall have a wee toast ;
Of which you may then have occasion to boast ;
     One hundred years to come !
This life is a warfare, (a sterling known fact ;)

* Psalm xlix.

In which, we as soldiers, have ceased to act ;
One hundred years to come !
The good fight of faith, let us fight, for the prize ;
Whereby we shall live, and eternally rise ;
One hundred years to come !
Hark ! " I am the first, and the last, saith the Lord ;
For Israel I fought," who has got his reward,
One hundred years to come !
For you I'll engage, if your trust be in me,
The God of all might : and for ever shall be,
One hundred years to come !
The thunder, and light'ning, with rain, hail, or snow ;
And the winds in a rage, or a tempest may blow,
One hundred years to come !
The Sun, and the Moon, and the Stars now so bright,
May all be dissolv'd in the darkness of night,
One hundred years to come !
But the promise is sure, you have it in hand ;
The word of the Lord, as a rock shall yet stand :
One hundred years to come !
The Saints who live on him, shall never more die ;
Hence they shall rejoice, in the wherefore and why,
One hundred years to come !
On the heights of sublimity, truly divine ;
As gems in the crown of their Author to shine :
One hundred years to come !
Then look on redemption ; and tell me, my friend,
If the blessings of grace, in glory shall end,
One hundred years to come !
If not, you shall sing of salvation for ever;
In the union of Christ, which nothing can sever,
One hundred years to come !

PART II.

Having pass'd, through this world, of trouble and care ;
And are verging the next, pray what's to do there ?
One hundred years to come !
Shall we live, and be happy, in Jesu's embrace ?
Or be damn'd with the Devil, in his horrid place,
One hundred years to come !
Let us now, think about it, ere time's at an end ;
That we all, may in heaven, eternity spend ;
One hundred years to come !
One moment of time, may this life terminate,
And unchangeably fix, our long future state ;
One hundred years to come !
Then, let us improve, the best talents we have ;
By the principle love, for there's none in the grave ;
One hundred years to come !
Lay hold of it quickly, enjoy, and maintain ;
The sweet comfort of which, shall ever remain,
One hundred years to come !
Perhaps you are saying, And where shall we keep it ?
That we may at present, and afterwards reap it,
One hundred years to come !
God's nature is love ; and a portion of which,
He'll place in your heart, if you want to be rich ;
One hundred years to come !
Sow your seed, in good ground, without any delay :
And the crop you shall reap, in the grand harvest day ;
One hundred years to come !
Ten thousand bright seasons, may pass beyond time ;
And yet be for ever, in yon happy clime !
One hundred years to come !

With angels, archangels, and seraphs, you'll sing,
Salvation to Jesus, (the Prince and the King :)
                One hundred years to come !
When millions of ages have rolled away ;
'Twill still but appear, as the rising of day :
                One hundred years to come !
And shall we be there then, with Jesus our Friend ?
Who, from the beginning, is world without end :
                One hundred years to come !

THE NATURAL MAN.

THE natural man is very weak,
    Tho' he may think he's strong ;
His arguments are good to break,
    By one small simple thong.
Grace, truth, or love, is that with which
    All wrongs are soon put right ;
'Twill make the poor in spirit rich,
    And set the crooked straight.
'Tis stronger than a world of things,
    When plac'd within the breast ;
And rises with ten thousand springs,
    To make man, truly blest !
Don't let him, in his lost estate,
    With logic pride ferment ;
Which bolts the door, and shuts the gate
    Of wisdom and content.
But let the man, with truth and grace,
    His reason exercise :

The candle then is in its place,
　　With light to make him wise!
Reverse the statement, if you like
　　To justify yourself;
Within you find a wretched tyke,
　　Or miserable elf!
The devil never could be worse,
　　Than what his children are;
Witness, the world's alarming curse,
　　Drinking, Bloodshed, and War!
The rod, was laid on nature's back,
　　When first she ran astray;
Which made a universal crack,
　　Heard, seen, and felt to-day!!—

MORAL.

Grace alone, must destroy the old man with his deeds,
　　That Nature in order may shine;
As a garden so beautiful, stript of its weeds,
　　Her principle then is divine!

SPEAK NOTHING AMISS OF THE DEAD.

SPEAK nothing amiss of the dead, my dear friend,
　　Because they are gone to the tomb;
Where the past is forgot, and with us should end,
　　Let them rest, poor creatures, at home.
Remember, that we must be there by and bye;
　　T' inherit a similar bed:

And folks will be talking of us, when we die ;
  Don't speak ought amiss of the dead !
Pray mind what you say of the dead, my dear friend !
  I tremble for those in the grave ;
And all my heart breathings to heaven ascend,
  That God would have mercy and save.—
Oh : that's it, my old friend, I see the design
  You have in a soft spoken word ;
Afraid the same epithet given, be thine,
  When the sound of the trumpet is heard !
Just listen a moment to what I advance,
  On the living, as well as the dead ;
Whose destiny settl'd, is not time and chance,
  Or a work of the comical head.
'Tis just as the talent we have is applied,
  While here upon earth we remain :
If mercy now tender'd to us, be denied,
  'Twill never be offer'd again !
Mark ! as the tree falls, so it lies on the ground ;
  Whether barren or fruitful, 'tis o'er !
Thus, the states of the living, will shortly be found,
  In judgment, as heretofore.
But why be afraid, now, to speak of the dead ?
  For they are a part of mankind,
Who, by the grim monster, to Jordan are led,
  And we, are the Pilgrims behind !
Posting on with all speed, a good staff in hand,
  Will support the weak and infirm ;
Till right 'cross the river, in Canaan we land,
  Having conquer'd the wind, and the storm !
Yet, the deeds of our lives, must ever remain.
  As patterns, or beacons to those ;

F

Who are yet on the stage, and wish to obtain
    Advantage, of friends or of foes.
We've Abraham, and Isaac, and Jacob on high,
    Bright stars of the first magnitude!
Whose light of example we cannot outvie,
    With knowledge, and virtue embued.
Manassah, and Magdala, glance at awhile;
    Tho' they, had occasion to mourn;
Who were fill'd with all evil, notoriously vile,
    Yet, by them a lesson we learn.
Were it not for the record of history, we
    Should be left in the dark on the past;
And the future, by faith, we never could see,
    The genius of man, would be fast.
Those reasons I publish, and heartily give,
    That others may profit thereby;
And now I exhort you, do right while you live,
    Then nought can be wrong, when you die.

MORAL.

Sheer truth is spoken by the dead;
    In tacit language, mark!
'Tis heard, and seen, and by us read,
    Though they, be in the dark!
But if their deeds on earth were good,
    More beautiful they shine;
Witness, the dear Redeemer's blood.
    In language all divine!

EXALTATION OF THE HUMBLE.

MANKIND, wide awake, do certainly know,
To rise up aloft, they must first be below ;
The humble and meek, submissive and kind,
Are never annoy'd by a turbulent mind ;
The path of the humble, is that of the just,
With brilliancy shining, according to trust :
Yea, brighter and brighter, in noble display,
Of graces and virtues, which cannot decay !
Thus, thus, are they bless'd, with a splendid estate,
And first class optimacy on them to wait :
With health, wealth, and pleasure, in store at command,
All which are reserv'd in the fair Promis'd Land.
Who exalteth himself, must certainly fall ;
But, he that is humble, possesses the whole :
And exceedingly more than I can detail,
In time, for eternity happen may fail,
T' disclose the vast splendour of glory above,
As the ocean is fill'd with immaculate love !
Pride, sprang from the devil ; and poverty, too ;
Tho', riches and fame, are designed for you ;
The humble in spirit, will shortly be known,
To claim all the kingdoms of earth for their own :
And the kingdom of heaven, through Jesus your friend ;
Shall be yours for ever, and world without end !

THE PHILOSOPHER'S STONE,
WISDOM AND KNOWLEDGE.

TRUE wisdom and knowledge are beautiful trees,
  On the which our happiness grows ;
Tho' knowledge beats wisdom ten thousand degrees,
  Where the fountain eternally flows !*
Yet wisdom alone, is the principal thing ;
  Nor was it design'd to be sold :
'Twill make the possessor delightfully sing
  Of riches, far better than gold !
What wisdom devises, true knowledge enjoys,
  Nor ever can run to decay;
The bright active intellect, always employs
  Itself, in the noble display !
True wisdom belongs, to the great King of Kings :
  By whom, the whole universe moves ;
For He, hath created the world, men, and things,
  But man, is the creature he loves !
A portion of wisdom, is given to him,
  Whereby, he may knowledge obtain ;
To keep the machinery, always in trim,
  That never wrought wisdom in vain.
To know the grand Author of all that is good.
  And " Jesus our friend, whom he sent ;"*
Is life everlasting, through His precious blood,
  The heart, and the seat of content.
A knowledge of men, and of things you may have,
  And never true wisdom obtain ;

* John xvii. 3.

If so, your deep knowledge, will sink in the grave,
    And all your own wisdom, is vain !
Then, know thine own self, man, in Jesus alone,
    If thou would self-knowledge possess :
For this is the only philosopher's stone,
    That increases, but never grows less !

THE FATHER OF SPIRITS, AND HIS CHOICE FAMILY.

THE Spirit of God, and the Spirit of Man,
    Are closely allied to each other,
By a deep philosophic and secret plan,
    Tho' felt, between brother, and brother.
The spirit of man, is a portion of God,
    Breath'd into his bosom at first ;
Whereby to attend the divine signal nod,
    To obey, and never be lost.
Thus holy, and happy, and lovely, and free,
    He stood, in the garden of love ;
Until he partook of the fruit of the tree
    Forbidden, then he had to move.
When, lo ! the perversion of right, was effected,
    He saw, and he felt it within ;
The eye of his Maker, that moment detected
    The crime, and behold it was sin !
The voice of the Spirit, was heard in the walk,
    Whereon the recipients trod ;

2 F

To whom was directed familiar talk,
    And that, was the language of God
At the sound of whose voice, conviction was made
    In the breasts, of the first sinning pair ;
By which the poor creatures, were sadly afraid,
    Nor could they be happy, while there !
Or fly from the Spirit, and Father of all ;
    Impossible 'tis, they have found :
Who heard so distinctly, the Master give call,
    And curse (for their sake,) the good ground,
On which grew the trees, so delightfully fair,
    Bearing fruit, deliciously grand ;
In the sunshine of grace, 'mid sweet balmy air,
    So long as they kept the command.
By the Spirit of God, engraven within
    The breast of each man upon earth,
To evince all the good, and the evil of sin,
    By the monitor given henceforth.
Yet, the beautiful garden, wherein they were plac'd,
    Is still as delightful as ever ;
To those, who will not see their land go to waste,
    But rule their own spirit so clever.
By the Spirit of Him, who hath given the same,
    To guide and conduct us below ;
And by the good principle, join'd to his name
    Whose nature, in love we shall know.
The Father, the Son, and the Spirit are one,
    A mystery none can define ;
So the spirit of man, in the body, or gone
    To the minist'ring spirits divine !
Our spirits on earth, do in harmony blend,
    And the Spirit of God we can feel ;

'Tis everywhere present, nor measure, nor end,
 But the Christian, bears the true seal.
By which to be known of his Father above,
 As the day of redemption, draws near;
Then the spirit (or soul) from earth shall remove,
 To know, what it cannot know here.
When matter decays, the freed spirit shall climb
 To mansions, which eye never saw!
Prepar'd for the holy, beyond space and time,
 To which, the soul flitting shall go.
Through Jesus alone, by the Spirit of whom,
 United are we, while on earth;
Altho' the vile body, descends to the tomb,
 The spirit obtains the new birth.
With Christ to unite, in the stature of man,
 And the likeness of God, to remain
In realms of bright glory, by his happy plan,
 And never know trouble again.
Adhere to the voice of this Spirit, my friend,
 Whose own you undoubtedly are;
And then you with Him, shall to heaven ascend,
 And shine as the bright morning star!

THE WHITE SHEET OF PAPER;
STRAIGHT LINES, AND GOOD CHARACTERS.

As a white sheet of Paper, was dignified man,
 So innocent, holy, and clear;
Sent into this world, with a rule, and a plan,
 To guide, and conduct him while here.

Let the first line you write, be perfectly straight,
  Then, in the same course you proceed;
With the pen in your hand, at your Author's command,
  Write characters, worthy to read.
In th' line of your conduct, I mean, you perceive;
  For if you but once get acrook'd,
Remember, Omniscience you cannot deceive,
  All deeds, good or evil, are book'd!
Preserve the white sheet, now, without spot or stain,
  Until you have fill'd up the same;
With pleasure you then look it over again,
  And sign at the bottom, your name.
'Tis a very bad job, if you once get awry,
  For the line you never can mend;
Altho', with self genius, you often may try,
  Yet crooked it stands to the end!
Disgrace and a torment, through life, to the man,
  Who has got but a sensitive mind;
To see he's perverted the rule, and the plan,
  And never another could find!
The white sheet of paper, was nearly lost!
  Mark, the subject I wrote with my pen,
Is a letter, which goes by the very next post,
  'Nor can it be written again!
The lily white sheet, to each one is given,
  With a portion of grace in the heart;
Which formeth the line, that leads unto heaven,
  From whence, we need never depart!

A DISSERTATION ON MAN.

MOST wonderful creature is man upon earth,
  Altho' he may seem left alone ;
With his Bride in conjunction, to levy their worth,
  Then tell me, for what they were born ?
To live here for ever, the youth would reply,
  And revel in pleasure below ;
God made us to live, but he knows the truth why,
  We shall, when to heaven we go !
The man full of business, would boastingly say,
  I'm healthy, and hearty, and strong ;
I'll work and I'll live, to enjoy my life's day,
  For it happen won't be, very long.
But the man full of years, perceives he must die ;
  Within his own system he feels,
What proves to him truly, in honest reply,
  To the blood, what the Spirit reveals.
Divine solemn facts, on the virtuous mind,
  Which nothing can ever erase ;
For the Author of Man, will always prove kind,
  To those who attend to his grace.
All the good things of time, that we can possess.
  Are talents we ought to improve ;
Then the Lord above all, will certainly bless
  Every deed, performed in love.
A true just account of the same, we must give,
  To the Judge of all men upon earth ;
And then we shall know, for what purpose we live,
  In the realization of worth.

And what have yon laid up in store for to use,
    When you have resigned your breath,
To the hands of your Maker? then listen to news
    Of the letter, arriv'd before death!
See, and know its contents, from the tongue of the wise,
    Who knows the end, from the beginning:
And truly just now, he will open the eyes
    Of those, who are free from all sinning.
Having shut up the vile, with worms in the grave,
    No more a disturber of peace;
We shall then the grand palm of true victory weave,
    Where glory shall ever increase!
Our business while here, we must duly perform,
    And then the enjoyment ensues;
At the end of our time, having braved the storm,
    When nature hath got all her dues.
The messenger Death, is no terror to those
    Who're standing in readiness now;
For the exit from hence, will triumphantly close
    Their doors, who submissively bow.
To the just, right, and wise, and holy decrees,
    Of the Lord, who does nothing wrong;
But kind to his children, the meanest he sees,
    And stoops oft, to sing them a song!
The last closing scene, upon earth, is the time,
    When angelic hosts do appear;
In splendoric vision, from yon happy clime,
    Of Glory, dispelling all fear!—
The grand panorama of time's at an end,
    Realities now shall appear;
And every beholder, along with his friend,
    Shall know, that his Maker is here!

Remember what's written, and profit thereby,
    For this, is the eve of the day ;
You put off your slippers, to mount up on high,
    And then, you shall tower away !
From all that is vile, and to all that is good,
    In splendid diversity given :
Without measure, or end, so well understood,
    By all the grand Orders of heaven !
As God is a Spirit, so we shall then be,
    Well clad in a suit of our own ;
Spun out, while in time, from the heart of the tree,
    The fruit of which, is as we've sown.
In a wee bit of time, the die will be cast,
    For ever, as such to remain ;
Nor can it be alter'd, those things which are past
    Must give, either pleasure or pain.
My epistle is come very nigh to an end,
    Nor are you at all in the dark ;
The voice which is speaking, is that of a friend,
    Who wishes you all to embark.
The scene has past over, and I must away,
    The Sun, is now on the decline ;
'Twill set by and bye, (in the close of the day,)
    And possibly never more shine.
A certain fair season, to each one is given,
    That all, may improve the grand store ;
Design'd by Jehovah, to land us in heaven,
    Which then, shall increase evermore !
The bliss everlasting, and glory superb,
    Surpasses, all language, or thought ;
Where nothing the peace of the happy disturb,
    Salvation, is then fully wrought.

The foretaste of which, is both yours and mine,
  To enjoy, as we're passing along;
While taught by the Spirit of Wisdom divine,
  Which teaches the harmonic song.
In the land of the living, where each recognize
  A brother, a sister, a friend,
In connection with Jesus, the elegant prize,
  We all shall obtain, in the end!
Yet, each have a business, or work upon hand,
  In which to engage, while below;
And press through the passage, to that happy land,
  Where Christians, are hoping to go.
Some people may travel by land, or by sea,
  On the ebb, or the flow of the tide;
While others are planting the green olive tree,
  The hand of the Lord doth provide!
He bids you go forward, attend to your duty,
  Nor harbour sad doubting or fear;
By faith, you shall see, the King in His beauty,
  When the light of His grace doth appear.
Then, leave the event, to the Father of all,
  Who gives us the sunshine and rain;
Impartially dealt, on the great and the small,
  That we, may the harvest obtain.
Attend to the Bible, act faith on the Word,
  Which never, no never, can fail;
Its virulent truths, you have felt, seen, and heard,
  In the voice of the whisp'ring gale;
Or the loud pealing thunder, terrific and grand,
  While lightnings so splendid appear!
The rainbow is set, by its Author's command,
  A token, to drive away fear.

And sweet indications of hope to impart,
　　To all who will trust in their friend;
Who gave the bright wheels of redemption a start,
　　Shall work, and prove true to the end.
The promise of God, in the centre we find,
　　To buoy up the heart in distress;
And give to the sickly, disconsolate mind,
　　A hearty, and welcome caress.
True comfort and peace, enjoyment, and all
　　The sweet consolations of grace;
Are given to those in a moment, who call
　　On Jesus, at this very place.
Then charmingly grand exultations arise,
　　In the breast of the sinner made free;
By the hand of true faith, he catches the prize,
　　And with its bright eye he can see!
All the winds, are one breeze, to waft us along
　　The ocean of turbulent time:
Until, on the calm, we shall sing the sweet song,
　　Of bliss, in a happier clime.
Till then, fare ye well, my dear kindred, and we
　　Shall soon meet in glory above:
Who are branches engrafted in that holy tree;
　　Whose nature, and fruit, are all love!

G

MOTIVES OF SYMPATHY.

DESPISE not the aged, the weak and infirm,
Whose pale furrow'd cheeks, are beat by
the storm,
Of poverty, pain, and distress :
The back-bent old man, with deep sunken eye,
And faltering tongue, will issue a cry,
That God, may the merciful bless.

He once was as young, blithe, cherry and fair,
As those buxom youths, plac'd under the care,
Of parents, or guardian friends :
Who tutor, instruct, and show them the way
To wisdom, and truth, in th' morning of day,
When God, with his blessing attends.

Compassion, goodwill, and sympathy must,
Well characterize, the path of the just,
Through life, and in every stage :
If we, the benefit want to receive,
The aged and poor we ought to relieve,
In charity's service engage.

The man with bald head, or locks very gray,
May have to regret his badly spent day,
And moan out a sorrowful ditty ;
Tho', sympathy must, rejoice and be glad,
To grant him relief, whose heart is so sad ;
For he, is an object of pity.

Time misimprov'd, has bereft him of powers,
And mark, by and bye, his case may be ours,
   Who look with contempt, or vile scorn :
And those in grand style, upon their estate,
May happen receive a rap on the pate,
   And be of their dignity shorn.

Afflictions may come, to rob you of health,
And spoil your fanci'd enjoyment of wealth,
   With silver and gold in your purse :
'Tis all of no use, to comfort your heart,
Your Idol, and you, must certainly part,
   When riches, have proved a curse.

A BRAVE AND NOBLE VICTORY, WITHOUT SLAUGHTER.

How rapid time passes, from youth to old age !
   The shadows of life are soon gone :
Those active Polylogists, now on the stage,
   Drop off, by the time they are on.

A dream of the night, or a vision by day,
   The genius of man will employ ;
In shifting the scenes, for the actors at play,
   While others may seem to enjoy.

A moment, at longest ; the vision is fled,
   And life's chequer'd scenes are no more ;

The humble, and haughty, have all gone to bed,
　　And quietly quitted their store.

A splendoric mansion ! or sweet little cot ;
　　The gold, and the silver, they leave
For others ; who them, will have shortly forgot ;
　　Delighted, with what they receive !

But what are we doing to benefit self,
　　As well as the rest of mankind :
Have we got the main treasure ? or gather'd up pelf,
　　Which flies, on the wings of the wind !—

Let the fair lily, (virtue ;) engage you while here,
　　Its benefit you shall obtain ;
When crossing the Jordan, there's nothing to fear,
　　You neither have sorrow, nor pain.

But cheerfully land in Canaan above,
　　T' enjoy all the treasures on high :
Reserv'd for you there ! in the fountain of love,
　　Which the wealth of the world, cannot buy.

'Tis Jesus ! the Lamb that was slain for our sin,
　　That we might partake of the tree :
(The fair Tree of Life ;) who the victory win,
　　For ever thrice happy shall be !

And short as life is, 'tis a warfare indeed,
　　In which we all have to engage ;
Mark, never kill time, or with it you shall bleed ;
　　And die, when you drop off the stage !

Then, take the small hint, that I gave you before,
　　And lay up your treasure on high ;
So when the grim monster hath shut to the door,
　　Brave victors, you live, when you die !

THE BIRTH, LIFE, AND DEATH OF HOPE!

THE contemplative mind is ever alive ;
　　With a prospect always in view :
And big with high fancy, in future, to thrive;
　　Or have the estate, made anew.

In anticipation of which, he can say,
　　While sat in the vortex of sorrow;
Altho', I am little or nothing to-day,
　　I hope to be something to-morrow.

This gem, in the breast, is a buoy to the mind;
　　Preventing a wreck on the shore ;
Possess what he may, and of whatever kind,
　　He hopes, for a far better store !

This privilege granted to man, above all
　　The beings created below :
Exalts his low spirits, 'mid trouble and thrall,
　　And helps him to jump, to and fro'.

Hope, springs up eternally, as we advance,
　　From youth, to decrepit old age :
2 c

Felicity thus, we may strive to enhance,
    While acting our part, on the stage!

This one thing is certain, that he who hath
        planted
    The comfort of hope, in man's breast:
Knew well, its sweet virtue, and gave what
        was wanted,
    To make the disconsolate blest.

In time, where alone it is needed, to be
    An anchor and stay to the soul:
When cast upon Jesus! the heart of the Tree—
    That blossoms, while ages may roll!

Then, hope in eternal fruition, must die;
    And faith, be interr'd by her side:
While charity answers the wherefore and why,
    A sample of which, we have tried.

THE WIDOW'S COMPLAINT: A PROFOUND SECRET!

AND didst thou leave thy mother's cot,
    My son, 'mid charms of youth?
Hast thou obtain'd a happier lot,
    Replete with love and truth?

Sometimes my fond caresses broke
 Thy infantine repose :
And then, I'd pass a pleasing joke,
 And kiss the lovely rose.

Dear boy ; when lull'd on mother's lap,
 I lov'd to see thee smile :
My hum would court the soothing nap,
 Devoid of artful guile.

The youth, grew jolly, blithe and fair ;
 In stature, nobly grand :
He was my hope, my joy, and heir,
 To all his Father's land !

But ah ! a change has taken place !
 The clay cold hand of death,
Has whiten'd all that blooming face,
 And stopp'd his fleeting breath.—

When fields were clad in verdant green,
 And Sol ; in lustre shone :
The years of John, were seventeen ;
 Thus, am I left alone.—

*   *   *   *   *   *   *   *

Except a sweet daughter, the hope of my age,
 But two or three summers ago ;
Since which, in her teens, (at a critical stage ;)
 Was Annie, bereft of her know !

The fine lovely damsel, a sweet virgin-rose,
 Which bloom'd in the garden, while young;
Instead of a comfort, enhances my woes,
 And silence sits now on her tongue.

When asking the "Dearie," if aught she may need,
 Not a word in reply do I get:
As a baby, I have the "Darling" to feed;
 And call her my sweet little pet.

Then I sit down to weep, with head on my hand,
 And ruminate o'er the affair;
Concluding, the "secret" I can't understand;
 My life, is all trouble and care.

May God of his infinite mercy draw near,
 And give me to see, feel, and know;
Why things so distressing to me do appear,
 A widow, deep sunken in woe.

"By and bye" thou shalt know, (but not down
  below,)
 The why, and the wherefore of this;
When Jesus appears, he shall dry up thy tears,
 And land thee, in heavenly bliss!

ADMIRATION, INTERROGATION, AND EXALTATION! THE STATE OF HEAVEN.

("WHAT MUST IT BE TO BE THERE?")

WE talk of the Canaan above!
　The land which the glorifi'd share!
Whose City, is built up in love!
　But, what must it be, to be there?

We talk, of the land of delight,
　So free from all trouble and care;
And the loveliest day, (without night;)
　But, what must it be, to be there?

We talk of the state of the blest,
　And the robes, they eternally wear;
In the Garden of Eden, possess'd:
　But, what must it be, to be there?

We talk of its sweet smelling flowers,
　(Situate, but we never saw where;)
In the charming, delectable bowers;
　But, what must it be, to be there?

We talk of the fruit-bearing trees,
　With flavour, delicious, and rare;
To be wafted in every breeze!
　But, what must it be, to be there?

By faith, we behold the good Land,
　With prospect, delightfully fair;
The enjoyment of which, is at hand!
　But, what must it be, to be there?

To partake of the whole with the King:
  And breathe, of the rich balmy air!
At the fount of the life giving spring,
  But, what must it be, to be there?

At home, with Christ Jesus, our friend!
  While here, let us each one, prepare:
That we, may to heaven ascend:
  And prove, what it is, to be there!

THE BREVITY OF HUMAN LIFE!

Not a man upon earth, can truthfully say,
  He is clear of mortal disease:
Terraqueous matter, must go to decay,
  And drop, as the leaves of the trees.

All flesh is but grass, that springs up in an hour,
  And dies, in a moment of time;
The scent of the rose, and the beautiful flower,
  Pass off, as the sound of a chime!

Or the winds of Boreas, which pass on the ear,
  Before you can speak, they are gone!
As a shadow that flies, so man doth appear,
  And never continues at one.—

Enquire of the pilgrim, whose day is far spent;
  He looks reminiscences o'er:
And tells you of seasons, how quickly they went,
  Creaking on, as the hinge of a door.

When he was a youth, full of action, and gay,
    The world was a fair lovely thing :
He joyfully pass'd the bright summer away,
    Then, all his sweet pleasures took wing!

Quite surpris'd is he now, to find himself old,
    With locks, white as new driven snow :
Quoth he, " I am cast in a comical mould,
    And chang'd by the winds as they blow.

The vari'd mutations, through which I have pass'd,
    From youth, to old age, now I see ;
Tho', never conceiv'd, while the summer did last,
    That winter was coming on me.

Old age has arriv'd, but I cannot tell how,
    From the first to the last, I may say ;
All quick as an arrow, shot off from the bow,
    So rapid has time pass'd away !"

One stream carries all, to the ocean from whence.
    The tide imperceptibly flows :
To its source, then returns and pitches man hence,
    (By every breath which he draws.)

To a new world discover'd, eternally new ;
    And a new set of people, you'll find
The old ones made over, as Jesus is true ;
    His children, he'll not leave behind !

THE ANCIENT BRIDGE OF TIME!
OR HUMAN LIFE.

ACROSS the bridge, where mortals pass
    The Isthmus of their day :
There is no passage, for the mass ;
    Or one, to slide away !
Across the vale of human life,
    This Ancient Bridge appears :
On which is found both care and strife,
    With many swords and spears !
The bridge, is common, to mankind ;
    And each, must pass along :
Not one, was ever left behind,
    Of all the mortal throng !
Ten thousand times ten thousand, now
    Are trav'ling on the way ;
Who hardly speak, or smile, or bow,
    Or nod, the time o' day.
High mounted, on their noble steed ;
    Or in the carriage ride :
Who think themselves, of splendid breed ;
    And rubbish, all beside !
While millions more, do trudge on foot,
    Or creep, from end to end ;
And often cast into the rut,
    Without a single friend !
Along the bridge of life, in time,'
    The strangest things appear :
While Apies, play the comic chime ;
    Hyænas, laugh and sneer !

Nevertheless, we mortals must,
   In duty, act our part ;
Set shoulder to the wheel, and thrust ;
   Or draw, the laden cart.
Perhaps you'd rather ride at ease,
   Along, the Bridge of Life ;
Thinking to catch a lovely breeze,
   Devoid of care and strife !
But, if with single eye, you take,
   A retrospective view ;
Your senses, then may be awake,
   To find the golden screw !
Deceptive, are the instruments,
   Made use of on the line ;
The box, with all its vague contents,
   Is partly yours, and mine.
As such, we can't expect to find,
   A plain, and easy way ;
While many, on the path, are blind,
   Who'er trav'ling, night and day.
The wise, the foolish, young, and old,
   The sick, the weak, and strong ;
The squeamish, lukewarm, hot and cold ;
   All nations, right or wrong.
Must, (like the Sun,) progression make,
   Without the least delay ;
Both day, and night ; asleep, or wake ;
   Nor can they miss their way.
The bridge, is broad, containing all,
   That ever liv'd on earth :
To high and low, to great and small,
   Our Captain cries, Come forth !

H

While, each one, hears, and sees, and feels,
  Th' imperative command :
Its Author, in the system seals,
  The truth, we understand !
Strange, weighty burdens, some will drag,
  Too heavy, to be borne ;
Before they reach the end, they fag,
  And of their strength, are shorn.
Terraqueous matter, is the weight,
  That presses all mankind :
At which they pull, with all their might ;
  And oft, against the wind !
Life's Bridge, is wisely thrown across,
  The two extremes of time ;
That man thereon might live, nor loss ;
  But find a better clime !
The Christian Pilgrim's final home,
  A rich, and wealthy place ;
Where earthly bundles cannot come,
  Tho' bound, with golden lace.
Upon the Bridge of Time, you see,
  By faith, the promis'd land :
Which bears the fruit of Christ, "the Tree :"
  That shall for ever stand !
Then, let us while we pass along,
  Be cheerful, blithe, and gay ;
With privilege to sing, the song,
  Of life, in endless day !
And realize, that blessed state,
  Beyond the Bridge of Time ;
The end of which, you'll find the gate,
  To yon, thrice happy clime !

Where, all the lovely Pilgrims meet,
  Their kindred, far and wide ;
In recipro, each other greet;
  And seat them, side by side !
Nor praise the Bridge, you got well o'er ;
  But let the praise be given :
To Jesus Christ for evermore,
  The Architect ; in heaven !

WHAT IS MAN ?

AND what is man ? a little thing,
  Plac'd on a clod of earth :
Which never could perfection bring,
  Beyond its native worth.
Then, is the appellation just,
  To one so imbecile :
Who sprang from out that bit of dust,
  To something mercantile ?
Altho' the structure of his frame,
  On principles divine ;
Would raise him to a higher name,
  And make his honor shine !
As when he bore the image of
  His Maker, and his God :
And then, his heart was fill'd with love,
  To animate the clod !
But what is man, since that took place,
  And has he lost the flame :

Which brighten'd up his lovely face,
  And stamp'd this honor'd name ?
A saint on earth ; bright, noble man :
  For Jesus Christ hath given
To him, by His redeeming plan ;
  A name, and place, in heaven !
The earthen vessel, now contains
  A portion of that treasure,
The bulk of which, with him remains,
  To be divulg'd, at pleasure.
Yet, notwithstanding this, the man,
  Who serves his Maker here ;
Shall have the title and the plan,
  His heavenly way to steer.
Through time, where men, and things shall end,
  The conquest then is o'er :
And man is chang'd, so like his Friend ;
  To reap the golden store !
And what is man, with all his parts
  Refin'd, and made anew ?
Soon as from earth the being starts
  With beatific view !
To range the boundless fields of bliss,
  Where nothing enters vile :
Nor can he ever fare amiss,
  With Jesu's lovely smile !

Queen Victoria's Proclamation,

IN UNISON WITH ALL HER SUBJECTS.

(NEUTRALITY IN WAR! MAY 1859.)

THE grand Proclamation of Peace, now is made,
  By Her Majesty, (Queen of the Realm ;)
Where honor and dignity, nobly parade,
  Victoria the First, at the helm !
Whose subjects are mighty, with wonderful power,
  To execute mercy and love :
Which all the vile characters, never can lower ;
  Or yet, the foundation remove.
The principal standard, hath conquer'd the world,
  By the light of the bright morning star :
The banner of Peace, in the " Lamb " is unfurl'd ;
  And this shall exterminate war !
The long wish'd for era, (which now is at hand,)
  More famous, than ever was known :
Shines through the dark vista, by sea, and by land,
  Where regions of bliss, are your own !
With the east and the west, the south and the north ;
  All Briton's in peace, do agree :
The grand proclamation of which, hath gone forth,
  From mind, Philanthropic and free !
Our hearts are rejoicing, delighted to hear,
  The musical sound of the voice :
Re-echo to Nations, (in love,) far and near,
  The object of Deity's choice !—

  2 H

When the hostile, in vengeance, and enmity meet,
  To cut, and destroy, one another :
We sit in neutrality's booth, to repeat
  The doctrine of love, to a brother !
Touch ye not the unclean, nor handle the vile ;
  Come out, from amongst the base clan :
And I will receive you,* with Victory's smile,
  In the dignifi'd Order of Man !

THE OLD ABBEY, OF GISBRO'.

WE speak of high towers, and the splendid remains
  Of Antiquities here, and there :
But look at Old Guisbro' ! " built up by the Danes,"
  When Christian heroes, were rare.
Behold the grand relic, an hundred feet high !
  (A splendoric stone window frame :)
On which the Jackalls, and the swallows do fly,
  The Owls, and the Bats, do the same.
While screeching, they gambol, and foster their young ;
  To the day, or the night passer by,
'Twould seem, as the voice, of an outlandish tongue,
  Grotesque, in peculiar cry.
The Monastry, once was held sacred, and free,
  To base superstition, and worse ;
They pluck'd the fruit off, from the best holy tree ;
  And then, would pronounce it a curse !
The Author, has fallen, to rise up no more ;
  Sheer vengeance, hath dropp'd on his head :

                  * II Corinthians, vi. 17.

The sword of true justice, is plung'd in the core ;
    And the Demon, has gone to his bed.
Who has left us a relic, the summit of which,
    Extends far beyond the dark cloud :
O'ershading the elegant seat of the rich,
    And fastens alone on the proud !
As blind as the Bat, that inhabits our bolt,
    Is the man, who will daringly say :
" Whom God hath forgiven, is still in the fault,"
    And yet, has his credit to pay.
The bolt of the Abbey, is all that is left,
    To tell where the Edifice stood :
Likewise to denote, how we all are bereft,
    Of parents, who welter'd in blood !
I refer you at once, to the Guisbro' star ;
    (I mean, the late John Walker Ord :)
Who, in his bright History, deprecates war,
    In unison yet, with the Lord.
The heart of humanity, feels for its own ;
    And Erebus never could give,
One spark of true light ; where the truth shall be known,
    The Gospel alone, bids you live !

SYMPATHY, DIGNIFIED !

WHILE musing, I feel in my bosom arise,
    The sympathy rarely we meet :
To th' ignorant, foolish, the learned, and wise ;
    Who can't with their betters compete.
The feeble, and wan, the sick, healthy, and strong,
    The aged, the halt, and the blind ;

Each and all have a part, or place in my song
    Of sympathy, due to mankind.
Yea, the rich, and the poor, the high, and the low,
    The beggar that lies at the gate;
Are subject alike, to the tempests that blow,
    In time; and may never abate.
'Till the mortal shall end, (the calm may succeed,)
    But let us have sympathy here:
T' all ranks, and conditions of men, in their need;
    And God will have mercy, no fear.
For he, in his dignity, never could gloze,
    Or pass the necessitous by:
Soon as he beheld us, his sympathy rose,
    And brought us relief from the sky!
Humanity honours its Author, with this
    Exemplication, in which
The sinner, is brought by the godly, to bliss;
    And the poor, are serv'd by the rich.
Who thus imitate their Creator on high,
    In principles solely divine;
Shall reap the reward of the just, by and bye;
    And with them eternally shine!
As stars of first magnitude, gems in the crown,
    Of all the rejoicings above:
Where Christ, is the centre of bliss, with His own,
    In sympathy, beauty, and love!

SUBLIMITY!

To lofty themes, our thoughts aspire ;
And strike afresh the golden lyre,
   With all th' angelic host !
Which, at Creation sounded high,
And rang throughout the vaulted sky,
   Supported by one post.

Till Christ appear'd, and made it three,
Extending wide the Deity :
   With grace, and glory too.
To lofty themes our thoughts aspire ;
Which kindle up the holy fire,
   In Christian hearts to glow.

And burn the dross of ancient days,
By hallelujahs to the praise
   Of Christ, the golden tree !
The King of Glory, Prince of Peace :
Whose vast dominions must increase,
   To all eternity !

From sea to sea, from shore to shore,
Till rising suns shall set no more,
   Our lofty themes shall swell !
And then, with songs the most sublime,
In yon thrice happy, lovely clime,
   Where every one fares well !

To lofty themes our thoughts aspire,
In realms of bright seraphic fire,
   For ever there to shine :

With angels, and archangels blend,
Our voices, which shall never end
The theme, of love divine !

THE CONTRAST!

THE trees in the wood, are all naked and bare,
And the birds in the forests are mute ;
The sheep on the mount, to the vallies repair ;
And Nature hath shifted her suit.
The lovely green pastures, on which they were fed,
Are nipt by the frost of the night :
And the herbage that bloom'd, is wither'd and dead,
Whereof they partook with delight.
When shepherds were tending their flocks on the green,
In the beautiful sunshine of May :
Ten thousand fair flowers, were then to be seen,
In silver, and golden array !
Sweet birds, all in harmony, chanting their song,
Delightfully charming to hear ;
No dissonant tone, nor a particle wrong,
And the rhythm of nature was clear.
The Sun, shone in splendour, and smil'd from on high,
On matter enliven'd below :
While grasses (retorting the smile of reply,)
Are stretching their hands as they grow !
Wherewith to receive, and acknowledge the gift,
Bestow'd by their excellent Friend ;
Whose life-giving beams, are all felt in the drift
Of bounty, which never can end !

And all this for man, who with gratitude can,
  Behold, and enjoy the grand store :
Where the table is spread, he may lift up his head,
  And feast on the same evermore.—
The contrast you have, between nature and grace,
  But cannot discern, till you find :
The sunbeams of Deity, brighten your face,
  And open the eyes of the blind.

A GOOD PRINCIPLE!

No pleasure have I, in abundance of things ;
  Let me have a competent store :
With contentment of heart, from whence are the springs,
  Which incline us to crave for no more.
The pressure of good things, will make them reverse ;
  And hamper us on with the slave :
Instead of the better, therewith we are worse,
  Than the fool, the madman, or knave !
Because of abundance, the heart cannot rest,
  Contentedly happy and free ;
The gratification of sense, is the pest ;
  Like the worm, at the root of a tree !
And thus, with the good things of life, we possess
  A heart full of trouble, and thrall :
For want of the grateful emotion, to bless,
  And praise, the kind giver of all.
With this requisition, whatever you have,
  No matter, the less, or the more ;

You've got the good heart, of the great, and the brave ;
　To give, with a never give o'er !
Perhaps you are saying, 'tis a very hard case ;
　We cannot give all that we've got :
Else, what in the world : we should not have a place ;
　Excepting the mendicant's cot !—
Thus you whiffle, and whine, and worrit yourself ;
　Altho' you have bread and to spare ;
You keep your old victuals, to waste on the shelf,
　While the poor, could do with a share.
" 'Tis godlike to give,* (and you cannot do more,)
　According to what you receive :"
Hereby to do good, with the whole of your store ;
　The wants of your neighbours relieve.

THE BARD INVOLVED !

KNEW a man, (a Yorkshire Bard,)
　Who, thirty years, had labour'd hard,
With sober industry and care ;
For this, and next world to prepare.
Tho', many a slip he made, 'tis true,
For which, (like others,) had to rue ;
And deprecate the want of grace,
To fix, and keep him, in his place ;
Whose nature vile, with passions strong,
Perplex'd, and held him in a throng ;
Tho', oft by others caught with guile,
Crep't on a foot, ran back a mile ;

　　　　* II Corinthians, c. 9.

Which kept him trudging many a day,
To gain what he had thrown away.
Nor ever could the same redeem,
Until he touch'd a higher theme;
With engine bright, the steam arose;
The guard gave whistle, off she goes:
With speed of Post, nor ever stays,
But hastens on, to better days.
Whose Railway is the length of time,
(And Station in yon upper clime;)
Where bliss eternal each obtain,
Who have their passport in the Train,
Shall cross the river Jordan, free,
And land in blest eternity!
No more to study, slave, and toil,
Nor ever burn the midnight oil,
With sleepless nights, and waking days,
To issue forth his Author's praise.
Free from the world's confused din,
With peace, and harmony within,
Devoid of anxious thought and care,
Thus tranquilliz'd, with prospect fair;
In subjects Godly, and sublime,
He spends his ever precious time.
Trusting the soul's expansion will,
Improve the store, and cash the bill;
Which, time well spent on earth, can pay,
And push him on to endless day.
Through faith in Christ, who laid the plan,
And thus redeem'd poor fallen man;
That we should to his glory live,
And then with him, new life receive;

I

By working talents he hath given,
To take us to himself in heaven.
And if our duty we fulfil,
For Christ's sake, God receipts the bill ;
The bill of fare, in passing through,
Which now from us to him is due.
Not that our works can pay at all,
What we inherit, by the fall ;
Yet, works and faith, do well combine,
To make our path, illustrious shine ;
And validate the blessings we,
Receive of Christ, who made us free.
To do his just commands, and live,
In charity with each, and give
A portion of that blessed store,
Which, while we grant, are getting more.
My talents then, may I improve,
And live in God, for God is love.

MORAL.

This privilege while, here on earth,
    If well improv'd, will shine :
As Gems of everlasting worth,
    In realms of light divine !
Never, no never, shall we rue,
    A life well spent in grace ;
For when to earth we bid adieu,
    In heaven we take our place.
Then, absent from the body we,
    Are present with the Lord ;
To live and reign eternally,
    And reap a grand reward.

What mortal eye can never see,
    Nor creature understand ;
'Till sever'd from the flesh we be,
    And in bright Canaan land.
To join the Tribes, who live and thrive,
    (But not on meagre fare ;)
With soul, and body, all alive,
    Breathing salubrious air !

THE PILGRIM'S PRAYER.

PART I.

JESUS, be thou, in youth, my stay ;
    In manhood, be my strength ;
Cast me not in my age away,
    When days have run their length.
Likewise when faint, and feeble grown,
    Support the aged sire :
Thy children, in the furnace own ;
    And screen them from the fire.
So, when afflictions, rage and swell ;
    They only may refine ;
And make the sickly patient, well,
    In grace and virtue, shine ;
Then, when those active limbs are weak,
    And these bright eyes grow dim ;
The balm, I need'nt have to seek,
    As I have all, in Him ;

Who, eyesight to the blind, doth give ;
   And strength unto the faint ;
When Jesus speaks, the dead shall live,
   The sinner, is a saint !
Old, meagre things, are done away,
   A new Creation springs ;
Darkness and night, are turn'd to day ;
   Subjects, are Priests and Kings !
This is thy 'mighty working power,
   Father of all above ;
Who sent to us the fairest flower !
   The essence of true love.
Whose sweet benignity, and grace,
   To all mankind extends :
For me, he hath prepar'd a place,
   Amongst his dearest friends.
I want to breathe thy spirit now,
   Tho' health, and strength decline ;
That I may in thy image grow,
   And in thy beauty shine !
Then, let the world, and things, recede ;
   Jesus, if mine thou art :
A friend I have, in time of need,
   With whom, shall never part.
When Jordan's raging billows roll,
   And on time's ocean lave ;
Thy peace, and grace, possess my soul,
   Convey'd beyond the grave !
To where the weary, are at rest ;
   The storms of life are o'er :
And I am then, most truly blest,
   In Christ, for evermore.

PART II.

WHILE on my Pilgrimage below,
    Within the vale of tears ;
Grant me, O Lord, thyself to know,
    Devoid of doubts and fears.
When storms arise, and tempests rage,
    Or pealing thunders roll :
Be thou my stay, from youth to age,
    Protect, and save my soul !
Altho', the tenement of clay,
    Shall drop into the dust ;
The vital spark, can not decay ;
    Decline, corrode, or rust.
In yon eternal house above,
    The place of sure resort ;
If fill'd, while here, with Christian love,
    Of which, the Building's wrought.
Secure on Christ, the Corner Stone ;
    The Rock of Ages, He !
Who did for all mankind atone,
    And life, he bought for me.
In youth and age, by truth and grace,
    In beauty, love, and peace ;
That faith, and hope, may reach the place,
    Where joy, can not decrease.
Nor pain, or sickness, ever come,
    Nor age, or death destroy ;
For we, shall be with Christ at home
    In life, and lasting joy.
For ever basking in the beams,
    Of His unsulli'd bliss :

And in that state, sing higher themes,
  Than e'er we sang in this.
And then, the sweet, and unknown rest,
  Which doth to those remain ;
Who, are in time, and ever blest,
  Shall still, increase the strain !

———

PEACE OF MIND OBTAINED, BY PROPER MEANS.

LET carping care, and anxious thought,
  Forever flee away ;
As dust before the wind, afloat
  In ruinous decay.
Or else, be sure they will disturb
  Your peace, and calm repose ;
For want of grace, wherewith to curb,
  Or quell, those inbred foes.
They're evils, of the vilest sort ;
  Base passions of the mind :
Not worth a Cockle, or a groat ;
  Then, give them to the wind,
They gender grief, and pain, and strife,
  When foster'd in the breast ;
And pester Man, throughout his life,
  Nor ever let him rest.
Sad doubt, and fear, and anxious care,
  Were never meant for man :
Who has to live, by faith and prayer ;
  God's own appointed plan !—

Lean on the arm Omnipotent;
  By faith in Christ, lay hold:
And he, will grant you sweet content,
  Within his lovely fold.
Who is the Shepherd, good and kind;
  In every point of view:
He leads the flock, that lags behind;
  To pastures, green and new!
Then, let all doubts, and fears be gone,
  And carping care subside:
By faith and hope, we travel on,
  For Jesus, doth provide!

THE GOOD OLD PILGRIM'S CAUTION, TO YOUTH.

THE aged Pilgrim now can see,
  What ne'er he saw before
The privilege of youth, which he
  In pieces sadly tore!
The gust of fancy, drove them hence;
  Borne on the wings of time:
Which carri'd off his own few pence,
  In nothing, but a chime!—
Time pass'd away, beyond his call,
  Nor would a moment stay;
By which he nearly lost his all,
  And threw himself away.
Careless, and inconsistent youth,
  Conceited, vile, and vain:

Will not attend to sterling truth,
  But falsehood, they retain.
'Till juvenality is past,
  And privileges fled ;
Then happen, they incline at last,
  To furnish heart and head.
When days, and weeks, and months, and years,
  Have slipp'd unheeded by ;
Suspicion comes, with doubts and fears,
  Of what they can't deny.
A few more rising suns, and then
  Our time on earth is spent !
Nor can we live it o'er again,
  Of evils to repent.
The man of years, (whose locks are grey,)
  With Jesus in his heart !
Like one of old, can truly say,
  I'm ready to depart.
And be with Christ, who liv'd and died ;
  But lives to die no more :
For he, did every good provide,
  I'll go, and reap the store.

MORAL.

In wisdom's ways, begin while young ;
  Take this advice, and live :
Were I to speak with Gabriel's tongue !
  No better could I give.

FAITH IN EXERCISE, AND ITS HAPPY RESULT.

GIVE, give to the winds, all your doubts, and your
    fears,
  Which only cause trouble and pain :
Dry up the big fountain, of sad briny tears ;
  Nor let them distress you again.

Or ever go mourning, and hanging your head,
  Like a bulrush, inclining to drop :
Remember the pastures, wherein you are fed !
  The staff of the Lord, is your prop.—

When faithful and trusty, you never need sink
  With burdens, no matter the weight :
As the chain is secure, in every link,
  And faith in the " Lamb," keeps it right.

Joy, peace, and true comfort, you then shall possess,
  Devoid of all trouble and care;
No need of forebodings of future distress,
  Your Father has bread, and to spare.

Rejoice in His name, put your trust in His word,
  Do your duty, as Christians here :
And stick to the truth, as before you have heard,
  You never, no never need fear.—

Calamities come to mankind, I'm aware,
  And often we meet them half-way :
With the vehicle Fancy, (the devil's old car,)
  Made use of, the same to convey.

Cast, cast to the winds, all your doubts, and your fears,
   Anxiety, trouble, and care ;
Shall then flee away, 'mid their own sorry tears,
   And sink in the pit of despair.—

Faith in Christ, is the hand, to cast the big mountain
   Of sin, with its sorrows, away ;
And in your fair bosom, 'twill open the fountain
   Of joy, that will never decay !—

A PARODY ON HUMAN NATURE.

HUMAN nature, in all, is the same,
   From the first, to the last, you will find,
Yet, the willing, may alter its frame,
   By a right, cultivation of mind.
As the issues of life, and of death,
   Do proceed from the heart of the man,
Who naturally bends to the earth,
   In the practise of which, he began.
Tho', the spark of true life, yet remains
   In the human, to raise the divine :
By the blood of Immanuel's veins,
   In his dignifi'd image to shine !—
You will find, human nature the same,
   Tho', 'tis held under better control :
When the spark, is well fann'd to a flame;
   'Tis a bright, intellectual soul !

But the statement first made, I contend,
  Human nature, is equal in all :
Yet, the last, will be first, in the end ;
  And the first, in oblivion fall !
We can never be equal and just,
  In a natural state upon earth :
Not a man, in the world, is to trust,
  As we all, go astray, from the birth.
Full of nought but deception and lies,
  Not a man, can in truth, say, I'm good ;
To the high, and the low, this applies,
  And by grace, it is well understood.
The possessors of which, cannot boast ;
  Tho', the hearts of the humble are pure :
They have nothing to spare, who have most,
  In the merits of Jesus secure.
Far beyond, what in verse, we can tell,
  Human nature, must go to decay :
Then, the super-divine, shall fare well ;
  In the sunshine of bliss, far away ! ! !

THE UNIVERSAL ROSE.

THE sweetest Rose, that ever bloom'd
  Where mortals live and die ;
Was sever'd by them, and entomb'd
  In dust, for you and I !
But mark ! its essence cannot die ;
  Throughout eternal day :

The crimson drops, do yet apply ;
　To wash, our sins away !
Love, is the virtue of the Rose,
　'Tis this alone can give ;
The union touch, to friends and foes,
　And make the dying, live.
Disease, of body, or of mind,
　No matter how impure :
The sick, the weak, the halt, the blind,
　In Jesus, find a cure !
He, is the Rose of Sharon, mark !
　The essence of true love :
Whose spirit, is the Vital Spark,
　To light the realms above.
With glory ! in unique display,
　Of which, the saints partake
While here, in part, but in that day ;
　Are fill'd, for Jesu's sake :
Who, surely is the best of friends !
　He died, and lives to prove ;
His fragrance, with our nature blends,
　And tells me, God is love !
This is the Rose : the only Rose :
　The sent of heaven, to earth :
Whereby to reconcile his foes,
　And give them all his worth !

A MISSIONARY SONG. ARISE, ARISE, ARISE!

ARISE, my mental powers;
   And taste, the sweets of life:
Which spring from out the lovely bowers
   Of peace, devoid of strife.

Arise my soul and shine,
   In yon bright world above;
Where Trees of Knowledge, are divine;
   And wisdom's fruit, is love!—

Arise thou morning star,
   On every opaque clime:
Go forth in love's majestic car,
   Ride, on the wings of time.

Arise, bright Sun, arise,
   On Nations far and wide;
Open all dark benighted eyes,
   Let ignorance subside.

Arise, both great and small,
   Let heathen lands rejoice:
In Jesus Christ, (who died for all,)
   And hear his charming voice!

Arise, ye dead in sin,
   From bondage you are free;

My Kingdom's open, enter in,
  Come, eat and drink with me.

Arise, and come away,
  Leave worldly things behind ;
Exchange your night, for endless day,
  And life eternal find !

Arise, arise, arise !
  And shine on earth below,
By works of love, you win the prize ;
  And faith, shall prove it so.

Arise, no more to fall,
  Christ Jesus, is your friend !
And with Him, you have all, in all,
  Where bliss, can never end.

MEMENTO OF THE POET'S BIRTH.

COMPOSED FEBRUARY 17, 1859.

WE calculate time, as it passes along ;
  And number the days of our life ;
The actions of which, be they right, or they wrong ;
  Are a medley of popular strife.
Just fifty-two years, I have been upon earth,
  This morning, ten minutes to eight :
While Sol, thro' the window, gave light on the birth ;
  The Baby, was surnamed Wright.

Who has spent the same number of years below,
 As are weeks, in a year, you'll find,
His anxiety is, by wisdom, to know
 The progress of soul, or of mind!
Which runs parallel with eternity's line,
 In evil, or good to remain:
As we live upon earth, hereafter we shine!
 If life, be without spot or stain.
The finger of God, having pointed the path,
 In which, while below, I should tread;
The kind hand of Providence, certainly hath,
 My feet, through intricacies led.
The arm of the Lord, with Omnipotent power,
 (Whose favour, is better than life;)
Hath been my defence, my safeguard and tower,
 In th' midst, of a world full of strife!
The garment unspotted, no man upon earth,
 Could ever produce by his deeds;
Filthy rags, at the best, and no better worth,
 Than gardens, all cover'd with weeds.
But, the unspotted life, was Jesu's alone!
 In whom, having faith, we are clean:
By the blood for us spilt, to wash and atone,
 And make us all, fit to be seen.
In the Kingdom of grace, and in glory above,
 With saints, and the angels of heaven:
Which nought in the universe ever can move;
 When once, the true vital is given!

FORGIVE YOUR ENEMIES!

Our enemies we must forgive,
  If we intend to be,
At peace with all mankind, and live
  To all eternity !
If not, mark well, they surely will
  Tormentors yet remain,
Beyond the bounds of time, and still
  Create, a deadly pain !
From which, we never can be free :
  The worm that never dies,
Will spoil the fruit, upon the tree,
  Wherever it applies.
But if fair Charity, within
  The lovely breast appear :
'Twill rid the heart of every sin,
  And make the conscience clear.
The fruit of which, is sweet and fine,
  Delicious to the taste :
The sun thereon, doth ever shine,
  Nor will it run to waste.
But if within the heart be hid,
  The least degree of evil :
Old Nickey, then, claps down the lid,
  We're box'd up with the Devil !*
"Vengeance is mine," saith God, "and I,
  Will certainly repay :"

* Psalm ix.

The soul that sins, must surely die,
 And wait the judgment day!
Mark, He is just, as well as good,
 Equal in everything:
And by the standard of His blood,
 Will all to justice bring!—
The best example ever given,
 To rebels such as we;
Was that, when Jesus purchas'd heaven,
 And died for you and me!
With His expiring breath He cries,
 " Father, I pray forgive,
The murderers of thy Son; who dies
 That they, may happy live!"—
Love, is the standard of our bliss;
 The fountain whence it flows:
True peace and comfort springs in this;
 And for the next world, grows!

THE REAL, AND IMAGINARY WANTS OF MAN.

THE real wants of man, are few;
 And easy to supply;
Tho', out of one, ten thousand grew!
 His whims to gratify.

However quick our wants may grow,
 By fancy's charming song;

2 K

"Man, needs but little, (while below,)
  Nor needs that little long."—

The one thing needful Mary chose :
  And that, with all her heart !
Whence, every good, and evil flows ;
  Which runs through every part.

A competence, is all we need,
  And that is made secure ;
When mortals to their ways take heed,
  With motive good, and pure.

Tho', nature calls out every day,
  For fresh supplies of bread :
Listen to what the Lord doth say ;
  How, are the ravens fed !

These have no house, wherein to store,
  The food, which God hath given ;
Yet, when they need, he gives them more,
  Supplies are sent from heaven !—

Were all the world in one estate,
  And by one man possess'd :
He'd want another quite as great,
  Nor yet, with it, be bless'd.

Our artificial wants are such,
  They cannot be supplied :
See, Alexander in the lurch ;
  When he, sat down and cried.

The heart of man, without content,
   Can never happy be :
With this, or that, which God hath sent,
   To set the captive free.

THE VIRGIN'S COMFORT.

THE honour, worth, and dignity,
   Of any single maid :
Depends on her benignity ;
   But not to retrograde.
The seal of joy, (devoid of strife ;)
   Shines bright within her breast,
Till made an honest, lovely wife,
   And then, she's truly blest.
If, to her equal she be yoked,
   A good-man, sweet, and fair :
Nor each by other, be provoked ;
   But every comfort share.
Happy, through life they now go on,*
   Thrice blest by God above :
Who first ordain'd them, two in one,
   Bound, by the cords of love !
With fecundity blest, to dwell
   In Jacob's hallow'd field :
Where every project, answers well ;†
   And fruits abundant yield !
Grace in the heart, " the Tree of Life ! "
   A progeny shall bear :

    * Proverbs xxxi. 10, 12.   † Psalm i.

As Isaac's charming, lovely wife ;
  The fruit of whom, we share !
Blest is the man, with quiver full
  Of those, who fear the Lord :
When each and all, together pull
  The gemy three-fold cord !
As plants they grow, that all may see
  The Poplars, tall and fair !
To flourish, as the green Bay Tree :
  Acknowledg'd, everywhere !—
Thus nurtur'd, in " the good old way ; "
  Wherein their Parents trod :
Shall make progression day by day,
  And scale the mount of God !
By good example while below,
  We rise superior far :
To those who don't the Saviour know,
  The bright and Morning Star ! !
Whose love alone, brought peace on earth ;
  And privilege to man,
While woman fair, enhanc'd its worth ;
  By, the redeeming plan !
You now perceive, why we have chose
  To dwell upon the theme :
That she, the fair and lovely rose,
  Doth merit man's esteem.
This privilege to her was given,
  With dignity and grace :
To bring forth Him. (" the child from heaven :")
  To save the human race !
This, is the gift of God alone :
  Confirm'd by nature's law,

Wherein, he was of woman born,
   That we himself might know.
The depth, and mystery of whom,
   We ne'er shall fully scan ;
Till pass'd beyond our native tomb,
   The privilege of man !—
Ye lovely fair, and virgin race,
   With whom the virile tribe,
Would join, and bring to sad disgrace,
   By some, alluring bribe :
Maintain your dignity, beyond
   The privilege of Man :
Or else your virtue will abscond ;
   And you are left a ban !—
Then, hold your grand possession, while
   You sing the matin song :
And you shall see the lovely smile,
   And hear the charming tongue !
Of him, whom God appoints for you,
   Wherewith to dwell in peace :
Through time, and then you reap your due ;
   Where love shall never cease !
Thus, blest in thought, in word, and deed ;
   Are those who Christ obey :
They till the ground, and sow their seed ;
   And wait, the harvest day !
The sun shines bright, while zephyrs fan,
   Their balmy, healthy breeze,
Throughout the privilege of man ;
   Enjoy it, if you please !

THE NAKEDNESS OF MAN.

A DISSERTATION.

NAKED, into this world we came,
    And naked must return ;
No matter what, our wealth or fame ;
    Nature's decrees are stern !—
'Tis said, that as we nothing brought ;
    Hence, nothing we can take :
But, stop awhile ; we're better taught :
    And should be wide awake !
Man, was design'd on earth to dwell,
    And work his own estate ;
By means which can't but answer well,
    Nor ever need abate.
And this, was given to him by
    His Maker. at his birth :
Wherewith, he nothing has to try,
    But, to increase its worth.
And that he'll carry with him when,
    And wheresoe'er he goes :
In spite of all the spleen of men,
    Or envy of his foes.
Then, tell me what and where withal,
    Man's best estate is found ?
And whether it be great or small,
    On swamp, or solid ground !
The principle, your Author gives,
    Who furnish'd you with eyes ;

To see, by whom the Creature lives,
   And know, by whom he dies!
'Tis this, the God of truth, and grace;
   Hath planted in the man:
A spark, which shines in Jesu's face!
   And wafted by his fan.
Thus, blown into a mighty flame,
   Which shall for ever shine;
With superb honour to His name,
   The Prince of Love divine!!—
Then, let us look th' estate around,
   Examine well, and try;
To see if principle be sound,
   On which we live, or die.
Hark! does the state of every mind,
   Sweet peace, and comfort bring?
Ah, no! some men acutely find,
   The lashing whip, and sting!
The day, my friend, is now far spent;
   Thy time, is nearly gone!
Of all thy former deeds repent,
   And put salvation on.
Thus, cloth'd in righteous robes, art thou;
   Nor age, or moth decay:
To Jesu's sceptre, humbly bow;
   This is the only way.
Tho', cursed was the ground at first,
   On which thy fathers trod:
Yet, Jesus gain'd, what Adam lost;
   And claim'd the seat of God!
Which, he hath promis'd unto thee,
   If thou obey His will:

While here on trial, short and free,
  Thy duty to fulfil.
" Thus, do to others, as you would
  Have others do to you ;"
Trust in the merits of His blood,
  And you shall never rue.
For, while on earth, you sow your seed,
  The fruit of which, you find ;
When blest in thought, in word, and deed,
  In body, and in mind.
The soul 's the principal of man,
  And occupies but clay ;
Wherein to work a certain plan,
  And then to pass away.
From earth, to some appointed place,
  And God alone knows where !
But, if prepar'd by Jesu's grace,
  We're sure to meet him there.
Then, all those goods are left behind,
  On which we set great store :
They're now as dust before the wind,
  Nor shall we need them more.
All we can hold, we keep within ;
  Nor with it ever part :
A clearance bill from every sin,
  And Jesus in the heart !
Example set, will always tell,
  A good, or evil story :
To lead its patrons down to hell ;
  Or up to endless glory.
If this be. true, then let us set
  The best example, while,

We have a chance as mortals, yet
　To make the sinner smile.
This is a legacy worth aught
　That we can leave behind :
Much better than the precept taught,
　To benefit mankind.
Mark ! this, is talent overplus ;
　Set forth, in grand display :
While others now, can learn of us ;
　And when we've pass'd away !
Moral example cannot die ;
　Altho' the man be dead :
He speaketh yet in sweet reply ;
　And lifts his honour'd head.
Exalted high, in those who live,
　And by their practice show ;
Something their fathers had to give,
　The fruit of which they grow.
" The naked clothe, the hungry feed,
　The destitute relieve ;"
This is the way to sow your seed,
　Only in Christ believe.
Who, knows the secrets of the heart,
　The passions of the mind ;
And every motive at the start ;
　To which He can't be blind !
Whose bright omniscience, is the light,
　Of nature, and of grace :
Shining throughout the darkest night ;
　At every time, and place !
Likewise His omnipresence doth,
　With His omnipotence,

L

In high majestic power go forth,
    And stand in our defence.
Against the wiles of every foe,
    And every vile attack :
His nod can break the lion's jaw,
    And drive the monster back !
Our strength, is in th' Almighty's arm ;
    Our safeguard, light, and tower :
In every storm, or bitter qualm ;
    And in an evil hour.—
If we can only shew the mark,
    Which all His children, bear ;
We're safe as Noe within the ark,
    And ride devoid of care !
Waters may toss, and seas may swell,
    While storms and tempests roar :
The voice within, cries, " all is well !
    I'll land you, on the shore !"
Faith realizes this, and can,
    Rejoice amid the storm :
As man is blest, by man, to man ;
    While confidence is firm !
Nation on nation, hangs secure ;
    In unity, they dwell :
When motives of the heart are pure,
    We each and all, fare well !
Tho' querimonious persons may,
    And will find fault awhile ;
Till squeamish passions fly away,
    Then, they begin to smile !
Why? because from head to foot they're clad,
    In one habiliment :

(Which makes the heart of nations glad ;)
   And that is, true content !
We say the heart, for all men's hearts,
   United are in one :
This is the way Millenium starts ;
   We hand in hand go on.
Ah ! could I see that blessed day ;
   When all mankind agree !
I'd spread one banner in the way ;
   To reach from sea to sea !
Its motto, " Love, and Peace on earth ;"
   To harmonize the world :
Our kings, and queens, shall feel the worth,
   And see the same unfurl'd !
In golden characters within,
   Exemplified without ;
A world of freedom, clear of sin !
   Which our Redeemer bought !
And Jesus, is His lovely name,
   Who died upon the tree !
The only Potentate of fame ;
   The King of kings is He !
Who rules the armies of the sky,
   And all the powers of earth :
Where truth, and justice, never die,
   And mercy, proves the worth ;
Of Him, who planted in the East :
   A garden, rich and fair :
Producing food, for man and beast ;
   (Mid sweet salubrious air !)
O'er which, he delegated man,
   To rule, and cultivate,

The ground, according to His plan,
   Who gave the grand estate!
With certain laws, and rules whereby,
   To regulate the whole :
" Do this and live, do that and die :
   By which, you stand, or fall.
Your will is free, you have your choice,
   To do my will, or not :"
But soon he heard his Maker's voice;
   Which drove him from the spot!
And then, himself quite naked found,
   Nor did he know before
The edict, " cursed is the ground,
   And thou art bless'd no more."
Poor Adam, and his wife, then walked
   In solitary maze :
And weeping, oft together talked
   Of former happy days!
" Mortal, my dear, are we become ;
   And die alike we must :"
The tongue of Eve, was nearly dumb!
   Who had betray'd her trust:
He, sympathizing said, " My love ;
   The seed of woman will,
In man, produce the God above,
   T' exonerate the bill!
Then, cloth'd in righteousness divine,
   We, beautiful and fair ;
Shall in the King's bright image shine ;
   The Father's Son, and Heir !"
Whom, he in mercy, freely gave,
   To take our sins away :

And raise us from the dusty grave,
  To live in endless day!

THE DEVIL'S SITUATION.

INTERLOCUTORY.

THE day of storm, we must endure,
  With patient resignation :
The same to quell, or work the cure,
  Which answers every station.
Troubles will come in every form,
  But don't be in alarm :
You know, a calm succeeds a storm ;
  Likewise a storm, a calm !
" Well well," say you, " but don't tell me :
  You haven't much to fear :
My bark is tossing on the sea ;
  She'll happen sink, this year !"
That may be true, the crew and all,
  May perish in this storm !
Then loudly now, for mercy call,
  And let your faith be firm.
But never doubt, in sad despair ;
  Jehovah, sits on high !
He, has your vessel under care,
  To whom you must apply.
Mark ! don't you say, " Lord, save my ship,"
  Omitting prayer for t'crew :
Or else, you make a horrid slip ;
  And you, shall have your due.

" But after all, she'd happen sink ;
   And then, I should be vext :
Faith's cable now has broke a link ;
   And what can you say next ?"
Your statement's just, perfectly just ;
   All confidence is gone ;
Nor could you in the " Captain" trust ;
   Alone, you sally on !
And if she sink, you cannot lay,
   The blame, on one, or other :
You must confess the truth, and say,
   " I've caus'd myself the bother."
In this dilemma, Peter was,
   While sinking on the sea :
Till doubting fell, (where faith arose,)
   And Jesus, set him free !
" Your waters, are too deep to wade ;
   Your thoughts too high to scan :
I must the subject now evade ;
   You know, man is but man."
" Yet deeper than the sea, I'll dive :
   And soar, beyond the sky !
To prove, that faith, is still alive ;
   Which made the devil fly
Away from happiness, to dwell,
   In torment, and despair :
And those who wish to see his cell ;
   Are sure to find him there

THE HAPPY MAN, IN SELF POSSESSION.

No foot of land do I possess,
    Or cottage of my own ;
While passing through this wilderness,
    Where pain and grief are known.
Nor will I with the world contend,
    For more than common fare ;
Nor time or talent vainly spend,
    In soul distressing care.
By diligence I must provide,
    For present daily bread ;
Then, future wants, are all supplied,
    By Him, who Israel fed.
The fertile land, on which we tread,
    The sea, on which we sail ;
Do each contribute to our bread,
    And water, cannot fail.
Long, as the Sun, and Moon endure,
    God's holy word maintains ;
The Bread of Life is made secure,
    In sweet Immanuel's veins !
The rustling wind, or gentle breeze.
    Which pass, o'er hill, and dale ;
Contribute to the growth of trees,
    Whose fruit, can never fail !
Likewise the orb of natural day,
    The silvery moon, by night ;
And all the stars, in grand display,
    Perform their work aright.

Not in advance, but at the time
　　Appointed them, they rise :
And each with light, and truth sublime,
　　Declare their Captain wise !
Instructing man, full well to know,
　　And do his work, while here :
Nor ever dare to look too low,
　　Nor yet too high appear.
Our privilege below is given,
　　(Exemplified above :)
By all the powers of earth and heaven ;
　　For God, to man, is love !
Then, shall I strive for house or land,
　　In all this vast creation :
Of which, my Father holds command ;
　　Appointing each their station ?
Content and happy, let me live ;
　　Nor for the world contend,
As Jesus Christ, has all to give,
　　And He's my only Friend !
A house in Him, I surely have ;
　　The title now is given :
That when I pass beyond the grave,
　　Will take me home to Heaven !

THE SWEET, SUBLIME, POETIC TREE.

IN Nature's grand Poetic field,
   Rich, spacious, and sublime :
Jewels, Parnassus' mount shall yield ;
   Throughout the length of time !
And nature's fertile plains below,
   In sweet abundance spread :
Where all her fruits so amply grow,
   On which the Muse is fed.
No famine can there ever be,
   The vine is always new :
Fine clusters set on every tree,
   Water'd by heaven's dew !
Altho' the streams from out the fount,
   Along the vallies glide :
Yet crystal drops, to any amount,
   Her fountains do provide.
Whose golden channels open are,
   Supplying creek and rill :
She rides in love's majestic car,
   Her mission to fulfil :—
To speak of all the varied store,
   With which she is replete :
Would open every mental pore,
   And fill Creation's sheet !
Capacious, as the universe,
   On which the mountain stands :
And issues, from the owner's purse,
   Who all the world commands !

Whose fund, can ne'er exhausted be ;
　　When time is worn away ;
'Twill last, to all eternity ;
　　More splendid in display !
A field, here opens, far and wide ;
　　Where suns immortal shine ;
On seas of bliss, with flowing tide ;
　　And principle divine !—
Here, fruits, and plants, and evergreens,
　　Perpetuate the scene :
Nor can compare where virtue reigns,
　　And runs through every vein !
Of every body, soul, and spirit,
　　Eclat in vital bliss :
The world above we must inherit,
　　Surpassing all in this !
Conceptive powers, however large,
　　Magnificent and bright :
Terraqueous things, can never charge
　　With permanent delight.
All are but similes of yon
　　Superb, unique display !
Without a jar, where every one
　　Shall harmonize the day.
Poetic strains, in language sweet,
　　And every line, a verse ;
And every saint, each word repeat,
　　And every soul rehearse !
Then, harmony shall ring, throughout
　　The broad expanse above :
And sing aloud, what Jesus bought,
　　With his redeeming love !

The living touchstone of the heart;
   And soul of Deity!
Which never can from him depart,
   The sweet " Poetic Tree ! "
Parnassus' streams, originate
   With him, the fount of peace :
Where life, and light, in happy state ;
   Shall evermore increase.
Love, joy, and purity, the fruit
   From that celestial Tree !
Shall all our mental powers recruit,
   Where every heart is free.
Here, then partake, and you shall live,
   In sweet salubrious air :
Where Jesus Christ has all to give,
   And you, shall meet him there !
Now, tune your harps on earth below,
   And then, in heaven above :
Where knowledge, truth, and wisdom grow ;
   With peace, and joy, and love !

THE SERENADE, WILLIAM AND ELIZABETH
1856.

As related to their Father, by Mr. James Milligan, who saw and
enjoyed the treat.

ONE fine lovely eve, in the spring of the year,
   On the which I was moving along ;
Sweet music, transporting, attracted my ear,
   By a flute, and the voice of a song.

Delightfully sounding, enchantingly sweet,
   In the grove, where I listen'd awhile,
To the harmonic strain, with love so replete;
   All Liv'rick* then issued a smile!
The musical birds, now in tune were engag'd,
   And myself with a heart full of glee;
Each at liberty here, nor fetter'd or cag'd,
   The somniferous treat, is all free!
While gazing around, I beheld the fair maid,
   Whose voice was transporting indeed;
Along with her brother, (and flute in parade,)
   Of Poetic family breed!
So sweet was the accent, and rhythm correct;
   The feet of the verse were all right:
Not a jar in the stanza, (that I could detect,)
   My senses were fill'd with delight!
The evening was calm, and the sky was serene,
   The rays of the sun were oblique;
The trees and the fields, bore an aspect of green,
   The treat I enjoy'd, was unique!—
'Twas the last sabbath evening this proved to be,
   That William e'er spent while at home;
Whose heart was inclin'd to pass over the sea,
   To the land of the West he would roam.
Left Father, and Mother, his Sisters, and all
   The grand scenery pictur'd above;
And cross'd the wide ocean, to stand or to fall,
   As a few passing years shall prove.
Tho' we sever on earth, where parting is pain,
   (To the sensitive breast of a mother;)

* A beautiful Wood near Roseberry Topping.

Yet, William shall see his dear sister again,
    And Lizzie shall meet with her brother.
Together with Parents, and Jesus, at home,
    If faithful to grace which is given :
Shall sound the sweet praises of his hallow'd name,
    And join in the chorus of heaven !
There, there we shall meet, in the land of the blest,
    And talk reminiscences o'er ;
Where all is unravell'd, and prov'd to be best,
    That was hid from us, heretofore.
Then, cheer up my friends, who are far, far away,
    Let nothing disturb you while here ;
The sun will soon shine, in the broad open day,
    And each, from all quarters appear !
Safe landed, at home, to rejoice evermore,
    With saints, and with angels above ;
In embrace of the "Lamb," (who hath sin for us bore,)
    The spring and the fountain of love !
What harmonic sounds, shall eternally ring,
    In the elegant vaultical space :
Where the sweet golden harps, are tuned by the king;
    To sing of salvation, and grace !
For ever and ever, and world without end,
    In musical concert to be :
With the angelic host, our voices to blend,
    Thus, perfectly happy, and free !

A GAME AT OLD LANG SYNE.

THE WINNER PAYS THE BILL.

Could I forget my youthful days,
    And not the past review;
I ne'er could sing the lovely lays,
    Which now I sing to you.
Sweet language in poetic strains,
    On themes so long ago;
Elate the mind while love remains,
    To witness truths we know.
When innocence dwelt in the breast,
    My heart would dance with glee;
A parent's voice pronounc'd me blest,
    And every thing was free!
Then, childhood ripen'd into youth,
    And I, ran too and fro;
In search of sentimental truth,
    Nor ever dreaded woe.
When guardians, faithful, just, and true,
    Where seated in the Dome;
They taught me what I ought to do,
    To make a happy home.
Those days are fled so far away,
    No more shall they return;
Tho', I have reach'd my longest day,
    I've lessons yet to learn!
A future day glides on apace,
    When time shall have an end!

Where shall I find my destin'd place;
  And where, my only Friend ?
In heaven I trust my rest shall be,
  When Jesus bids me come;
To dwell with Him, (for ever free,)
  And all my charge at home.
Then, then " the days of Old Lang Syne,"
  Shall I recount with pleasure ;
And call the past, and present mine,
  An endless lovely treasure !
A boundless store the future has,
  For me to realize !
But not to pore on what I was,
  'Tis here, the secret lies !
" Buy up the moments, as they pass;
  Enjoy the present day :
If not, your happy hours (alas !)
  Are all fled far away !
And then, the retrospective glance,
  Will not rejoice the heart ;
Nor yet your future bliss enhance,
  You sold it at the mart !
Where sin, and folly, pride, and shame,
  With vast ignoble skill ;
Got you to play the woful game,
  " The winner pays the bill !"

THE OLD MAN'S DEMONSTRATION,
SALVATION OBTAINED IN THE ELEVENTH HOUR.

NEGLECTED duty while in youth,
 Is torment in mid-life;
Old age thereby is press'd with grief,
 With trouble and with strife.
This mighty burden, might have pass'd,
 When youth was strong to bear,
But now the feeble back doth bend,
 With sorrow, and with care.
His golden days are flown away,
 Sweet youth, and manhood fled;
Nor can recall one single deed,
 To crown his hoary head!
Anon while on the close of life,
 He casts a languid eye,
Where spring was fair, and summer bright;
 But now, they've both gone by!
From three, " to three score years and ten,
 Our life is but a span :"
The retrospective glance will tell,
 This truth to mortal man.
Behold him sitting, meand'ring o'er
 The follies of the past!
With flut'ring heart pulsations move,
 And soon will beat their last.
But ah! the startling thought: what then?
 Ah! when the spirit's fled

From this clay tenement below,
  Cast, in its native bed !
Am I prepar'd to meet the change,
  Which shortly must take place ?
Ah ! had I listen'd to the voice,
  Which sounded gospel grace ;
My peace might as a river, been
  Flowing, with ebbing tide
Of mortal life, and as she wears ;
  Eternal life provide !
But ah ! the spring, and summer's gone !
  I'm left an aged tree :
With neither fruit, nor blossom fair ;
  Dear Lord : remember me !
I do regret my time mispent,
  My folly and my sin ;
Open the door of mercy, pray,
  And let the sinner in.
I know, thou didst for sinners bleed :
  By faith, the Cross I see !
Pray, help an old man, nigh the grave ;
  Dear Lord, remember me !
My head is bald, my beard is grey,
  My back is bent with age :
And all the elements of time,
  Against my soul engage.
My day is spent, the night is on,
  While raging tempests beat ;
And shake the cottage made clay,
  Nor can I hold my feet.
The Rock, the Rock, the Rock I want ;
  Which tow'rs amid the whole !

2 M

Unmov'd, secure, and stands the test,
  When tabernacles fall.
Hide me within its cleft, dear Lord ;
  And then, the swelling tide
May rage, and foam, but can't devour ;
  I've Jesus on my side !
" Thou hast the words of endless life,
  Ah ! whither should I go ?"
Now speak the word, that I may hear ;
  And feel, and see, and know.
My staff I'll drop, and lean on Thee ;
  Jesus, the Lamb of God :
For Thou alone, can set me free ;
  By Thine atoning blood !
Hark, hark ! I hear the rushing wind :
  Hark ! 'tis the Spirit's voice !
I hear the sound of pardon come ;
  Which makes my heart rejoice.
Now, now I feel my burden gone ;
  And I have peace within :
My Saviour hath the blessing given,
  And cancell'd all my sin !
A flood of grateful tears burst forth ;
  These furrow'd cheeks to fill :
My heart rebounded, when I saw ;
  Jesus, discharge my bill !
Glory to Him, for evermore ;
  Glory to God on high :
Across the Jordan now I'll pass*
  Triumphant to the sky !

* Satur Dierum.

Thence shouting vict'ry, on the verge
   Of an immortal state :
Of happiness, or endless bliss,
   Tho', very nigh too late !

———

A DIALOGUE;

BETWEEN AN OLD MAN, AND A YOUNG PRIEST.

FRIENDLY INTERCOURSE.

WELL well, old friend ; and whither bound,
   So aged and infirm ?
Your head seems bending to the ground ;
   Whence sprang the feeble worm !

Yes, yes, young man, your statement's just,
   And I shall shortly lay
This weary body in the dust,
   To moulder and decay.

Well well, old friend, but that's not all ;
   An answer I desire :
You may be in the midst of thrall,
   And some small aid require.

That's very kind, young man, indeed,
   With supposition true ;
And tho' assistance I may need,
   Perhaps I've got my due.

How so ? the aged and the poor,
   Demand our sympathy ;
Who have to beg from door to door,
   And cry, " remember me !"

I'm sure young man, you hit me hard,
   And yet I can't but say ;
My life will merit no reward,
   Let me trudge on my way.

Stop, stop, old friend, another word
   I wish to have with you ;
A better subject I have heard,
   And you must hear it too.

Subjects enow, I think I've got,
   For many, many years ;
Through life, I've had a tedious lot
   Of hopes, and doubts, and fears.

Well, well, those days are gone, and fled !
   No more shall they return :
Lift up your hoary, drooping head ;
   Man wasn't made to mourn !

I thought he had, I'm sure I did :
   I've mourn'd so much myself ;
And often said, (tho' God forbid,)
   That man was like an elf.

Man, makes himself a mourning thing,
   Beneath his dignity :

Contrary to our heavenly King ;
    And what He did decree.

Ah yes, but when I thus reflect,
    And view a mispent life :
Then, all my errors I detect,
    In turbulential strife !

Well, well, but this is not the way
    To mend a life mispent :
You must without the least delay,
    Believe, and then repent.

Methinks I do repent, young man !
    Could I live o'er again,
I'd never take the course I've ran ;
    But life, and bliss obtain.

The soul, extramundane must rise,
    From all terraqueous things ;
Through grace alone, surmount the skies,
    Whence, true salvation springs.

You speak of what I never knew,
    Altho' I've sometimes heard ;
While sitting in our old Church Pew,
    Scarce understood a word.

Ah ! that's the evil, I suspect,
    By which you miss your way ;
The mercy offer'd, you reject ;
    And spend your time in play.

But now, no time have I to play,
   So I'll be trudging on ;
And bid you kindly sir, good day ;
   Perhaps, your lecture's done ?

Ah, no, it isn't yet, old friend ;
   I've something more to say :
And trust you will to me attend,
   Then, I'll move on my way.

Thank · you, kind sir; and I'll give ear
   To what you've got to say ;
Tho' I've to sweat, and toil in fear,
   While on my far spent day.

No toil, or exudations will
   Disturb your calm repose ;
When all the wheels of life are still,
   And time, with you shall close !

Well, never mind, just let me go
   To earn my daily bread ;
For that's the staff of life you know,
   To prop the hoary head.

So far, so good, but that's not all !
   A better prop you need :
Your tabernacle soon must fall,
   On which the worms shall feed.

You seem as tho' you knew the whole,
   Of what will happen me ;

Tho' but a Poplar young and tall ;
    And I'm an aged tree !

The tree is by its fruit well known ;
    Likewise are all mankind :
And every one shall reap his own,
    Of body and of mind.

Tho' aged and infirm you are,
    Yet Christ can make you new ;
For He, the bright and Morning Star !
    Shall give to all their due.

The guide of youth, and manhood's strength ;
    The staff of hoary age :
Till time with us, hath run its length,
    All this, did He engage.

And now old friend, farewell, good bye ;
    For youth and age must part :
We'll live, and love, until we die ;
    Tho' you have got the start.

THE SUNSHINE AND SHADE.

(A PASTORAL.)

THE Sun of Prosperity shone for a while,
    On the plants, and the shrubs, in the vale;
Where blossoms, and roses, protend their sweet smile,
    And we, in the centre regale.

The trees of the wood are all lovely and gay,
    Drest up in their fine olive-green :
While lambkins are jocund, and merrily play,
    The morning is calm, and serene !
Sweet zephyrs are plying their wings of perfume,
    Refreshing in every breeze :
The landscape is deck'd in its verdant costume,
    With musical birds, on the trees !
Rejoicing to witness the beautiful morn,
    They issue the harmonic sound ;
While dewdrops of crystal, upon the Hawthorn,
    Are shaken, and fall to the ground.
On the soft silky moss, and the fine tender grass,
    With herbage nutritious and sweet ;
O'er which, all the Cattle in jollity pass ;
    And partake of the excellent treat.
Methinks, while I'm gazing thereon with delight,
    The beautiful prospect is mine :
To enjoy the repast, with an intellect bright,
    And sentiment, wholly divine !
Comparing vast nature, with virtue and grace,
    Transcendantly higher than all ;
We behold the reflection of Jesu's bright face,
    And hear, His sweet life-giving call !
In language (tho' tacit,) emphatic and true,
    " See, Children ; my table is spread :
With everything lovely, sweet, handsome, and new,
    Your Father is sat, at the head !"
The sunshine of grace, beaming forth in your heart,
    From the Orb of spiritual day :
Shall never more set in the west, or depart ;
    As a shadow, that passeth away.

But, right in perpetual motion 'twill keep,
    The secret, (which never was known,)
Shall then be reveal'd : as we sow, we shall reap ;
    And each, have a crop of his own.
The sunshine and shade my dear friends, are the things,
    I wish to impress on your mind ;
The former, shall dignify subjects, and kings ;
    The latter, will cast them behind.
I need not dilate on the form of the shade,
    'Twill only increase the dark cast ;
What cannot give pleasure, I like to evade,
    And ward off, the cold bitter blast.
The extremes of the case, you may happen perceive ;
    Then, bask in the rays of the sun :
On the bright Sun of Righteousness, only believe ;
    And your shining, will never be done !
For ever and ever, while ages may roll ;
    As stars of the first magnitude :
In lustreic transport, of body and soul,
    You're happy, with glory embued !
All the day, (without night,) nor a vestige be there,
    Of aught to o'ershadow your bliss ;
Then, haste to the spot, by faith, hope, and prayer ;
    Through Jesus alone, you have this !

N

PRIVILEGE OF THE SAINT, ON DEPARTING
THIS LIFE.

" The chamber where the good man meets his fate,
  Is privileged beyond the common walk of virtuous life;
     Quite in the verge of heaven!
  Whatever farce the boastful hero plays,
  Virtue alone is majesty in death."—YOUNG.

THE scene of Death, no one can paint
  Correctly, with the pen ;
Tho', Pope and Baxter, show the Saint
  Departing, lives again !
Did not our Saviour dying, live ;
  And prove it, the third day ?
The first fruits of His Church to give,
  Infallible display !
My Mother's soul is tow'ring high,
  Tho', on the verge of death ;
She now beholds her Saviour nigh,
  Witness her dying breath !
Whose eyes gaze on her offspring dear,
  Collected round her bed ;
Who wait the whisp'ring sound to hear,
  Before her spirit's fled.
Then, calling each one by their name,
  Said, " Children, do not mourn ;
Into this world I naked came,
  And naked must return.
I'm going, bless the Lord ; I see,
  Angels around me stand !

And Jesus Christ, who saith to me,
    ' Sister, stretch forth thine hand !'
Conduct my spirit, Lord, I pray ;
    To Canaan's happy land !
I'm bound to go, without delay,
    Jesus, at thy command !
Farewell, my children, fare ye well ;
    Dear husband, farewell too ;
Be good and kind to each, and tell
    Your friends, I'm made anew !
Poor father, must be left behind ;
    To act, apart from me :
Attend this admonition kind ;
    ' In union all agree.'
Until the call for you is given,
    Which I shall now obey ;
On wings of love I'll soar to heaven,
    Away, away, away !
Ah ! gone, a little on the start ;
    Whence, you may shortly come :
But, strive for purity of heart,
    And we shall meet at home !' ''

MORAL.

This is the scene to contemplate !
    Which none can understand :
Until they realize the state,
    And join the spirit band !

THE SEVEN STAGES OF HUMAN LIFE;

IN THE SEVEN AGES OF MAN.

In the first stage, I hung on my dear mother's breast,
　My heart seem'd in sorrow to beat;
Yet, sooth'd by her balsamic kisses to rest,
　I enjoy'd the infantine treat.
The Baby was laid in the cradle to sleep,
　Ma', look'd on its angelic face:
And breath'd the sweet prayer, that Jesus would keep,
　Her offspring, for ever in grace!
Then Boyhood arriv'd, when I smiled to see,
　The trinkets presented to view:
All nature was charming, and lovely to me;
　With every thing honest, and true!
To th' rosebud of Youth I advanc'd, full of glee;
　Nor pester'd with trouble or care:
All blooming, and bright as the green holly tree;
　Ah! wasn't it good to be there?
In retrospect often I'd look on the same;
　And wish for the day to return:
Wherein I was happy, amid the bright flame
　Of love, in the bosom to burn!
Thus, to manhood I rose, as the poplar tall;
　With passions prospective, and high:
Not thinking the leaf, with the blossom may fall;
　Or man, in the morning, may die!
The fourth stage I enter'd, elated to see
　A world full of secular folk!
And I, with a partner so active and free,
　Engag'd, in the conjugal walk.

What one thing an' other, (to tell you the whole,)
 Transpiring in this stage, would fill
A sheet seven acres ! to scribble the scroll,
 And make out the comical bill.
The fifth stage I notice, is solid and grave ;
 When wisdom is got, if at all :
By experience, which characterizes the brave,
 And keeps him aloft at the fall !
As Autumn arrives in the sixth stage of life,
 Man's leaf must now wither away :
His glory shall fade in mortality's strife :
 And nature, pass on to decay !
The seventh and last stage, of life is at hand :
 And if I have fought the good fight :
My course is now finish'd ! by Jesu's command,
 I'll pass off the stage, with delight !
As here, (in the midst of the whole) I have found
 A Pearl, the grand Author of seven :
My foot is well fixed on good solid ground,
 I'll pass through the ordeal, to heaven !

MORAL.

Both Childhood and Youth, are in Vanity Fair;
 Mankind in mid-life are the same :
Except they of wisdom lay hold, and take care
 In Youth,* not to tarnish their name.

* Ecclesiastes xii.

A PRACTICAL DEFINITION OF THE SEVEN AGES OF MAN.

1st.—Infancy, Seven Months.

2nd.—Childhood, Seven Years.

3rd.—Boyhood, to Puberty, Fourteen Years.

4th.—Youth, to Twenty-one Years.

5th.—Manhood, to Forty-two Years.

6th.—Zenith stage, to Forty-nine Years.

7th.—Declination, to Seventy Years, the allotted Age of Man! thence, with patriarchal strength, the old man may progress, but mark, he dies!

This is a remarkable fact, that at the end of every seven years of human life, there is a radical change in the physical system, which is acknowledged by the connoisseurs of every age, and verified in the experience of mankind to the latest period of time! the secret movings of which, mysterious are to us ; and ever shall remain, well known alone to Him, with whom we have to do, whose mighty workings were at first, in secret wrought ; the hidden source of which, our Father still retains, to carry out His wondrous scheme of Nature, and of Grace ! ! !

· Ordain'd by wisdom : King of kings !
   'Tis Thee ! Omnipotent divine ! ! !
Tho' hid, are all thy secret springs :
   Yet, grace throughout doth truly shine.
Both soul, and body are restor'd,
   Through death, grim death ! to life again ;
Witness, the passage of my Lord !
   By which, eternal bliss obtain.

A SWEET SOLILOQUY.

ALL verdant in the rise of youth, is man;
 While blooming nature, wears her lovely dress;
And zephyrs waft their odorif'rous fan,
　In healthy breezes ; we the balm caress.
And then the matin notes, peal forth in songs
　Delightful, from the Lark on sprightly wing,
Soaring aloft : where harmony belongs ;
　And issued thence, the hills and vallies ring !
Melodious reverie ! purity and grace !
　With no designing maxim, ever drawn ;
To blight the bud, or mar the lovely face,
　Which shines resplendent, on the vernal morn !
But, ah ! like leaves, the race of man is found :
　Tho' green in youth, must wither on the stem,
And fall in Autumn, to their native ground,
　Where nought survives, except the Vital Gem !
Matur'd, preserv'd, and now hath taken flight ;
　Far from chill Winter's blast, with tempest drear;
To one perpetual Spring, on Zion's height :
　And there to breathe the holy atmosphere !
Where trees of righteousness, shall ever grow,
　To bloom, and blossom, in immortal youth :
Nor imbecility, or langour know,
　'Mid all the splendours of, unerring truth !

A GLANCE ON FORMER DAYS.

ON the sweet spring of youth, with rapture I gaze!
  And anxiously wish the return:
Wherein, to improve all the prime of my days,
  And practical lessons to learn.
When life, and high spirits, pervaded my breast,
  The scene was transporting indeed!
Phantasmas of pleasure, in beauty were dress'd;
  On which, the bare fancy to feed.
In lovely green pastures, of plenty and peace,
  Where fiction, was taken for truth;
The mind bound in fetters, ne'er sought for release,
  Mid pleasure, and pastime of youth!
The juvenile days of the past I review,
  And fain would recall what is fled:
But no, to my youth, I must now bid adieu;
  And the tear of sympathy shed.
Yet I cannot but look, at the years gone by,
  And the comforts, I once did enjoy;
From which interdicted, in vain I may try,
  The days of my youth to decoy.
They're fled, as the zephyrs, that fly in the morn,
  Preceding the sunshine of May!
Tho' sweet as the honey, from off the hawthorn,
  So artfully stolen away.
A shadow, a cloud, on the bright azure sky;
  An arrow, that's shot through the air;
With rapidity flies, at the quirk of an eye,
  'Tis gone, but you cannot tell where!

All my past time is fled, but the deeds of the same,
    Are written indelibly sure :
With letters emboss'd, in the characters' name ;
    Eternally now, to endure !
Yet, I cannot but look, on the days which are fled,
    So pleasing, and lovely were they :
The tear of reflection, again I will shed,
    On the friends of my youth, far away !
Who are pass'd off the stage, on the wings of old time,
    Will never, no never, return :
'Tis well for the parties, in yon happy clime ;
    Whose lamps, do eternally burn !
But, I look and admire, the days of my youth,
    When spent in the sunshine of grace ;
Where virtue, and honesty, wisdom, and truth :
    In the heart of the young, have a place.
As jewels of silver, in apples of gold,
    Those juvenile characters are ;
Who're plac'd in the front, for the world to behold,
    And follow the bright morning star !
In th' pathway of duty, with pleasing delight,
    Where safety is ever within ;
The life of the just, is the sun in the night !
    Dispelling the darkness of sin.
The past, and the present, are charming to see :
    Where virtue, and truth, are combin'd :
The subject of which, is a fine fruitful tree !
    To those of the dignified mind.

POPULAR VARIETY.

God, seems to love variety :
 Witness the grand display
Of Mortals, in society ;
 And faces, every way !
Nor two alike, of human kind,
 Were ever known to live ;
Equal in body, or in mind ;
 But, this is God's, to give.
And in the large Quadruped race,
 Variety is seen ;
Tho' he appoints to some, a place
 Where Man, has never been.
Witness the Fishes in the sea,
 Of every shape and size :
Then count the vast variety ;
 With wonder and surprise !
The Feather'd Tribe, can waft their wing,
 Between the earth, and sky :
With varied notes, their sonnet sing ;
 And each, to each reply.
On vegetative matter gaze !
 The Shrub, the Plant, the Tree ;
And every blade of Grass, displays
 The sweet variety !
And all the Flowers that ever grew
 To ornament the ground :
Present their varied aspect, new
 To all the world around !

The rippling Rill, the flowing Tide,
   The Ocean's rapid move!
Ne'er can diversity subside,
   While God alone, is love!
As stars of various magnitude,
   Which stud yon canopy:
So are the gems of mind imbued,
   To write their epopee!
Both men and things, in every stage
   Of human life, do vary;
In Childhood, Youth, and hoary Age;
   They seem as all contrary.
Thus, in a world of constant change,
   No wonder if we see,
Terraqueous matter, on the range,
   In great variety.
Mark! multiplicity of mind,
   So varied in degree;
Demands a section, for each kind;
   To form society.
The Foot, the Leg, the Arm, the Head;
   Are members of the frame;
And by one heart they all are fed,
   But each a different name.
Yet, all may harmonize, and sing
   The same essential song:
As streams do from the fountain spring,
   To which they all belong.
This, is the grand, triennial joint,
   Uniting every limb:
Within the Body, at the point,
   Where nought is out of trim!

Let sects, and parties, all agree
   In Christ, (their living Head,)
To think, and act, as ever free,
   And by His Spirit led.
Then each, at length, shall rise and shine,
   In magnitude to vary :
As stars, and suns, yet all divine !
   Where nothing is contrary.

THE TIME-PIECE OF HUMAN LIFE.

RAY, Father, tell me what's the Clock
   Of human life you see :
And where's the hammer fixt to knock
   The bell, that rings in me ?
Likewise the pointer on the hand,
   Which tells the time o' day ;
And never stops, by sea or land,
   Till life has pass'd away.
" My Child, when you are Seven years old,
   'Tis One o'Clock with you ;
Your lot is cast within the mould,
   Where you have work to do.
The Clock strikes Two, at Fourteen years,
   You're qualified to act ;
Mid sorrow, cares, and doubts, and fears,
   The mind is often rack'd.
At Twenty-one, 'tis Three o'Clock,
   To Manhood you are come ;

Collect together all your stock,
   And make yourself a home.
When you arrive at Twenty-eight,
   'Tis Four o'Clock, my man!
Now, you must strive with all your might,
   To work the golden plan!
'Tis Five o'Clock, at Thirty-five,
   Your dial must be clean;
And every faculty alive,
   But not an action mean.
At Forty-two, it's Six o'Clock:
   The flower is fully blown!
And all your flax is on the rock,
   To spin, and work your own.
But when your years are Forty-nine,
   The Bell rings loudly seven:
The Sun of Life has cross'd the line,
   The Equinox is given!
That man may calculate, and find
   At Fifty-six, 'tis Eight:
The Clock of Time, is thus inclin'd
   To turn his day, to night!
At Sixty-three, the Bell rings Nine;
   And peals, with solemn sound:
As life, and health, are on decline,
   You're bending to the ground!
At Seventy years, the Clock strikes Ten;
   Th' allotted age of man:
Whose mental eyes begin to ken,
   His life, is but a span!
And if you reach to Seventy-seven,
   (At which my father died;)

o

The Clock of Time, has struck Eleven,
　　And life will soon subside.
But if you live to Eighty-four,
　　The Clock strikes Twelve in truth ;
Then, earth shall open wide the door,
　　And let you in forsooth.
The Time-piece now is worn away,
　　The wheels of life are still ;
Thrice happy he, who spends his day,
　　Obedient to God's will.

MORAL TO THE TIME-PIECE.

THE full age of man, I have counted, but hark !
　　The Time-piece may never strike One ;
Until the whole system be left in the dark,
　　And the breath of vitality gone !
Then, the Bell of Eternity rings in the ear,
　　Of those who are left on the stage !
Where tumult and trouble, distraction and fear,
　　Disturb us in youth, or in age.
But one thing essential, each have to attend,
　　Let the Clock move on as it may :
Secure an int'rest, in Jesus your Friend !
　　And then, you're at right time o' day.

A QUERY.

RAY, who can speak the truth, and say,
This world is all a bite?
So much 'tis practis'd every day,
And seems our sole delight.
Those who are dealing with mankind,
Are selfish in degree:
For when they judge their neighbour blind,
Do fancy they can see!
Of whom, will take advantage, then
Their weakness is the prey;
On which they ply themselves, as men
Who rob, without delay.
This villany through life is seen,
And felt in every stage;
The principle in youth, tho' green,
Is ripe in hoary age!

———

THE PRODIGAL'S PICTURESQUE RETURN.

EHOLD, the Prodigal return!
And see him puff and pant:
In full exertion now, to learn
The lesson taught by want.
His heart beats high with sentiment,
Submissive and sublime:

As he could never find content,
　Far, in a foreign clime!
His eyes are fix'd upon the mount:
　The Morning Star appears!
And floods of water from the fount,
　Descend in bulbous tears.
The penitential flag is out,
　The Father sees the sign:
And runs to stop the waterspout,
　With message all divine!
He knew the features of his child,
　And recognis'd his son:
Altho' for years he wander'd, wild;
　Till all he had, was done.
And now appears in tatter'd clothes,
　All destitute and wan:
But stript of which, the Father knows
　The value of the man!
With all agility he sped,
　And ran to meet his son:
Who, long had been the same as dead;
　But now reviv'd, and won!
The complicated smart he felt,
　The keen pathetic touch:
Which prostrate threw him, as he knelt,
　Pathosity is such!
The Father: fell upon the neck
　Of his beloved child:
And kiss'd the Prodigal, a wreck
　No more by sin defiled!
Then, up they rose, in converse sweet;
　And posted on their way;

To where the family shall meet,
    And spend a joyful day !
The Father's house, is now in view ;
    To which he'll soon repair :
Tho' once he bid the whole adieu,
    No more of it to share.
The Father with the son, arrives !
    And all, quite safe and well :
Tho' envy, at the sight connives ;
    Love, rings the music bell !
Strike up your golden harps, and sound
    This sweet and charming note !
" The dead's alive, the lost is found :
    Salvation's scheme is wrought !
Prepare the feast, for he shall eat,
    And drink with me to-day !
And you with us shall have a treat ;
    Make ready, don't delay.
He's stript of all his rags and dirt,
    Yea, wash'd so sweet and clean :
And cover'd with a bran new shirt :
    Equal to king or queen !
A ring is plac'd upon his hand,
    New shoes upon his feet ;
And here the Prodigal doth stand,
    The story to repeat ! ! !"

THE ARDENT REQUEST OF THE VENERABLE SAGE.

Now, when I am old, and grey headed, dear Lord :
    Be thou the support of my age :
The faltering ebbings of life, can afford
    No comfort on earth, to the sage !
Give me grace to submit in the evening of day,
    To the wisdom of infinite love ;
By the wings of whose purity, borne far away,
    On the pinions of faith to remove.
From the terrene abode, of the tenement here,
    Whose structure is on the decline ;
Fast crumbling to dust, and shall leave in the rear,
    All nature, except the divine !
Proceeding with joy, to the heavenly goal
    Of happiness, high in degree :
Where portions of which, to the great and the small,
    In justice, allotted shall be.
So now, when I'm old, and grey headed, be thou
    The staff of my age, to the end :
That when nature fails, in the valley below,
    My spirit to thee may ascend.
There join the society, happy and free
    From the changes, and chances of time ;
Where dignified orders, for ever agree
    In sentiment, wholly sublime !
Then, sickness, and death, grief, sorrow, and pain ;
    Are fled, and eternally gone :
Fair youth, health, and beauty, for ever obtain,
    The old, and the young, are as one !

THE CHRISTIAN'S CONFIDENCE; AND THE HAPPY RESULT!

Tho' famine, poverty, and pain,
   In desolation spread ;
Yet faith in Christ, shall me sustain,
   And lift my drooping head.
Tho', clouds and howling tempests rise
   Terrific, while below ;
I have a house above the skies,
   And faith, shall prove it so.
Tho', stormy winds, with bitter blast,
   Attack, with pelting hail :
I'll keep my courage to the last,
   And weather out the gale.
Tho', light'nings glare, with vivid flash,
   And pealing thunders roll !
While castles, rocks, and cities crash,
   I'm safe amid the whole ;
Shelter'd beneath th' Almighty's wing,
   Shall laugh, and smiling cry,
" Salvation to the lovely King !"
   And all the world defy !
My soul ; trust thou in providence,
   Tho' things contrary seem ;
Blessings on those, he will dispense,
   Who're high, in His esteem !
Altho' the Fig Tree blossom not ;*
   Nor fruit be in the vine :

Habukkuk iii. 17, 18.

Jesus himself is on the spot!
  Whose children cannot pine.
The Olive labour, chance may fail;
  The fields may yield no meat:
Yet, Jesu's kindness doth prevail,
  Which makes the bitter sweet.
The flocks, be sever'd from the fold,
  Nor herd, be in the stall;
Still, let thy confidence be bold,
  And thou, shalt never fall!
By faith, my trust is in the Lord,
  In whom I will rejoice:
For there, is all my treasure stor'd,
  And He's my only choice!
Mark! no good thing will he withhold
  From thee, a child of grace:
Thou art a lamb, within the fold!
  Thy Shepherd's in the place!
And He'll take care of thee, no doubt;
  The Father, loves His child:
Nor will He ever turn thee out;
  Or cast thee on the wild.
Only attend the Master's voice,
  Nor ever run astray;
And thou shalt evermore rejoice,
  Throughout the happy day!

THE HAPPY RESULT.

WHEN the lovely green pastures are open to thee,
  And the sweet flowing Kedron, so wide ;
In the fair promis'd land, delightfully free ;
  Thou shalt bathe, in the sylvanic tide !
Of celestial glory : in oceans of bliss,
  With luminous seraphs to shine ;
In the bright worlds above ; (more splendid than this ;)
  With satellites solely divine !
Deliciously grand, to contemplate awhile ;
  And breathe, a wee gust of the air ;
In the wilderness here, with Christ's placid smile,
  But, what must it be, to be there ?
In the land of the blest, eternally so :
  Nor ever be sever'd again ;
From those, whom we lov'd, and enjoy'd, while below ;
  Who with us, shall ever remain !
Ten thousand times happier than any conceive ;
  The foretaste of which, we have here :
But if, by the pledge, you have faith to believe ;
  Reality, soon shall appear !
And when you arrive at your own destination,
  Through Jesus ; you'll sing the new song :
Compos'd by himself, (in the scheme of salvation,)
  To whom, all the praises belong !
Holy armies comprise, the saturnian band ;
  With music, transportingly sweet :
Who range the fair plains, of the thrice happy land ;
  Enjoying, the splendoric treat !

For ever and aye ; yea, and world without end :
　　As ages eternally roll :
In the chariot of love, you ride with your friend :
　　Possess'd of new body, and soul !

———

A QUERY ANSWERED, VIZ :—WHAT IS THE SOUL ?

WHAT is the human soul, in man ?
　　　　A splendid world divine :
A something, mind can never scan,
　　While clods the Gem enshrine !
What is the soul : pray tell me friend ?
　　A spark of heavenly flame :
Which in its origin shall blend,
　　And bear its Author's name !
What is the soul : I want to know ?
　　And measure its degree :
This, thou can never do, below ;
　　Nor in, eternity !
Then, shan't I know, as I am known,
　　By Him, who made the world ?
When I am master of my own,
　　Won't it, be then unfurl'd ?
Oh yes, but when shall that appear ?
　　The soul of man, is such,
It knows but very little here ;
　　And yet, may know too much.

Unless its Author do control,
  And regulate the mind ;
The mysterious world ! (the human soul :)
  Its nature cannot find.
Much less, the unlimited extent,
  To which, shall ever soar :
If God's own Son, give thee content ;
  Thou'll ask for nothing more !
And ah ! to feel the christian soul :
  A world of bliss within ;
Which cannot fail, while ages roll,
  For ever void of sin !
If thou can tell me, what God is :
  I'll tell thee, what is man :
Who seems to be a probing quiz,
  To know more than he can.
Tho', if he did, himself but know ;
  He wouldn't be far short,
Of knowing everything below ;
  That wisdom ever taught.
The soul's origin ; tell me that ?
  The Sun of Righteousness :
Which on our nature, brooding sat,
  Determin'd, man to bless !
Who, at the first, was nothing more
  Than dust upon the earth ;
Moulded behind, likewise before,
  Till Spirit gave him breath.
And that was God ! (the Holy One,)
  Fill'd, with celestial fire !
From whom, a single spark has gone,
  To animate the mire.

Then, man became a living soul,
   And co-eternal with
The Tree of Life : (while ages roll !)
   Tho', Jesus, is the pith !
In whom, the Godhead, now doth shine,
   Replete, with truth and grace :
Whose grand munificence divine,
   Gave mind, a local place !
And dost thou want, some more to know ?
   Then let the Spirit's fan ;
Upon thy spirit ever blow :
   And that's the soul of man !
And are we thus, so near allied,
   To Him, the God above ?
That nought can sep'rate, or divide,
   The christian soul from love !*
Yes, this is truth, you can't deny ;
   Nor should I vaunting strive :
Tho' some, inhuman brutes will try,
   At virtue, to connive.
And bring it down, to things created ;
   O'er which, they have control :
To whom, their body is related ;
   But not the human soul !
These, these are things sublime, and grand ;
   Beyond conceptive power :
Which mortals, cannot understand ;
   Or yet, their standard lower.
Jesus, will tell you, bye and bye ;
   What you can never know :

Romans viii. 38, 39.

Till on the wings of love you fly,
   By faith, from all below!
What I have said above, you'll find,
   In sweet eurithmy clad :
To raise the weak desponding mind,
   And make the valiant glad—
To feel the source of every good,
   Within their bosom burn ;
Which makes my subject understood,
   " Man wasn't made to mourn."
But, to rejoice in everything,
   And give to God the praise ;
Who is the fountain and the spring,
   Of all our happy days !
A world of glory is the soul,
   Only in Jesu's name :
Then let us dip into His bowl,
   And now enjoy the same.
Bethesda's pool, salvation's streams,
   Rivers of grace are free :
For all, (whom Jesu's blood redeems,)
   No matter who they be !
Then, may I from His arms ne'er sever,
   But in His image rise :
To whom be all the praise for ever,
   Amen, my soul replies.

THE SPIRIT WORLD REVEALED.

THE ARGUMENT.

WERE all this universe of matter, in which we now
exist; bound to lay in one chaotic mass, as in its
pristine state; devoid of spirit, life, or action; and
but one bright spirit peeping through the chink of
innate lustre, on all the dark and dismal scenery below,
in worse than ruinous decay; without one soul, or
spirit, to animate the bulk, which of itself could not
give light, or action; tho' in the midst of an ethereal
space: which some would vainly, and presuming say,
is life of all. But tell me whence that judgment came
by which vain man decides? could all or any part of
this big bulk of lumber, create one particle of lovely
light to shine amid the darkness now prevailing? no
never, never, never. But the eye of flame, with arm
omnipotent, and wisdom without end; knowledge
superb, and love divine: which, brooding with his
spirit, on the same, caused all, at once to live! whose
voice gave echo, and electrified the mass, which into
being sprang, with beauty, and magnificence at
once! then order first in matter got a start: and
lovely nature, with her charming scenery began! and
man; most noble creature! then was made, out of
this lumber, with soul, and spirit given, to rule all
minor things of God's creation. For he alone is
that bright eye, of which we speak! dependent upon
none; at whose sole will and word, all things do
now exist; and ever shall, by absolute authority;

which none shall e'er control; though some pre-
sumptive beings, (vile, base ignoramuses) will contend
and strive against their Maker; as he himself declares; who is the life, and soul of all! I scarce
dare touch upon their mean and low insinuation, (viz.)
"ether is the soul, or spirit!" What ignorance is manifest in this expression! The element in which it
does or may exist, (as far as we can see, with vision
wisely limited,) they designate the soul! I envy
not their mind, who think the body, is the soul; and
soul is wind! Perhaps it would be well for such, if
theirs were nothing else. We grant, man's mortal
life is as the wind which passeth off, so brief; but
where is the soul, or thinking part of man? and
whither has the spirit fled? Into a world as yet
unknown to man: absent from the body, but present
with the Lord! Mysterious is the Spirit World!
Let daring man be silent here, and stand in reveren-
tial awe of God! nor grieve His Holy Spirit!

WHEN, in the stillness of the night,
　　Beneath the azure skies:
'Mid darkness bound, (nor needing light,)
　　Asleep my body lies!
And yet, the spirit tow'ring high;
　　Rides swift, on eagle's wing:
To both extremes of earth, will fly,
　　And home, some message bring.
While all my senses are asleep,
　　The spirit is awake:
Around the world, 'twill have a peep;
　　And thus, its pleasure take.

Anon, it flies across the seas,
    (Where we, have never been ;)
And perches on, yon foreign trees,
    Or capers, on the green.
She flirts along, to friends afar,
    And joins in conversation ;
With tribes at peace, or tribes at war ;
    No matter, what their station.
Sanctum, sanctorum of its God ;
    Beyond the bounds of time :
'Mid tracks of ether, never trod,
    'Twill rise to things sublime.
There, in angelic company,
    Delighted, join their song :
And raise the sweetest symphony,
    With more than Gabriel's tongue !
Thus happy, is the spirit when,
    The body is asleep ;
Until it do return again,
    Its mortal house to keep.
A few short days, or months, or years ;
    At most, and death will sever,
What has been join'd, with doubts, and fears ;
    Shall be at rest, for ever !
Tho', long she wander'd here below,
    'Mid seas of discontent ;
Where bitter blasts, tempestuous blow ;
    And sound, their deep lament !
Asleep, or wake, 'tis all as one ;
    The active spirit must,
Alike engage, when life is gone,
    And left the mortal dust !

God is a spirit ! what has man,
  Within his house of clay ?
Here, let him grip' tight as he can,
  The spirit flies away !
Thus, pass'd into the " spirit world !"
  (Its native element :)
Where things mysterious, are unfurl'd ;
  To breathe, a sweet content !
Mutations, on this shifting stage,
  In altercations, pace
The paths of life, from youth to age,
  Nor spirit in one place !
Immanuel, is its Author's name ;
  And God with us shall be :
As now, and ever, just the same,
  To all eternity !
A portion, of the Holy Spirit ;
  Alone to man, is given :
That he, may with the Lamb, inherit
  Glory : reveal'd in heaven !
Come then, to this bright spirit world ;
  And feed upon the store,
Salvation ; is my theme unfurl'd,
  Come, drink for evermore !
Here, light, and life, and truth, and grace ;
  In streams of crimson dye ;
Shine forth in Jesu's lovely face ;
  In torrents from on high !
As waters do the ocean fill ;
  'Twill spread, from sea to sea :
Then, every river, brook and rill ;
  Shall in one fountain be !

2 P

Return'd for ever, to the source,
  From whence, our spirits rise :
By love's attraction, (not by force ;)
  This spirit, never dies !
Witness the " Lamb : " who took his flight,
  From Calv'ry's rugged mount !
Rising victorious, by the light,
  To yon most splendid fount !
From whence all life, and beauty came,
  With everlasting love !
" Father of Lights," (in Jesu's name,)
  The King : enthron'd above !
Christ in you now,* who sent his spirit,
  To testify on earth :
That we, His glory, shall inherit ;
  The spirit's second birth !
The spirit world, (on which I treat ;)
  Mortals can never scan ;
Except their hearts, with love shall beat ;
  And sound, the God in man !
The spirit, tries the spirit, bound
  With matter while below ;
And in the breast of man, 'tis found
  To wander to and fro.
In vague, and mythy worlds we be,
  Engaged more or less ;
Striving to handle, chace, or see,
  Some spirit in distress !
Those seem delighted when they find
  A chink, or flaw, within

* Collossians i. 27.

The Christian heart, (or man of mind ;)
  Who deprecates their sin.
Tho' striving to enhance the worth,
  Of that poor blinded spirit ;
In heaps of dust, and clods of earth,
  Nor will the light inherit.
According to the spirit which,
  You manifest yourself ;
In this world, are you poor or rich ;
  A saint, or churlish elf !
And in the spirit world shall be,
  Just as we act in this ;
Throughout a vast eternity,
  Our woe ; or endless bliss !
Are not they all, who bask in beams,
  Where suns immortal shine :
Now, minist'ring to us, on themes
  Of glorious light divine ?*
High, and exalted, tho' they be,
  Yet unperceiv'd do fly ;
From shore to shore, from sea to sea :
  And here, are thousands nigh !
With message, from the spirit world !
  Of mercy, love, and peace ;
Which fully, cannot be unfurl'd,
  Till mortal life shall cease.
And yet, their watch, and guardian care,
  Is manifest, while here ;
O'er kindred spirits, every where,
  In this world, far and near !

* Hebrews, i. 14.

Nor day, nor night, debars them from,
    Their philanthropic work;
Ordain'd by him who bids all come,
    To where no spirits lurk!
In gloomy shade, or passage dark,
    Or deep obscurity:
For God's omniscience, is the spark,
    That shines, in you and me!
By whose bright eye, (the holy spirit;)
    Attendance shall be given:
To light, and guard, (through Jesu's merit;)
    The spirits, bound for heaven!
With God to dwell, who is the spirit,
    Thrice holy, just, and true:
Whose bliss, the saints shall all inherit;
    Through Christ, the golden screw!
Tho' thousands here, may wander wide;
    Far from the central point:
But when at home, nought can divide,
    The splendid treble joint!
Uniting all angelic powers;
    With spirits of the just;
Made perfect here, and why not ours!
    Embodied, in the dust.
Ten thousand times ten thousand, now
    In caskets made of clay;
Are exercis'd, but tell me how
    They work, from day to day?
In this vast busy world of mould,
    Terraqueous things engage
Our spirits, (which are faint, or bold;)
    From youth, to hoary age.

Alternate, in the cumbrous clay,
　　Wherewith, are clog'd on earth;
Tho' flick'ring much to tower away,
　　To things of nobler worth.
The spirit world beneath the sun,
　　Exerts herself in vain,
To get her finite business done;
　　Infinite bliss to gain.
As such, are hoarding up in store,
　　A vast of worldly pelf:
In expectation, less or more,
　　T' enjoy it all herself!
But, ah! the human cannot live,
　　(And thrive,) on bread alone:
Superior food, the Lord doth give,
　　To those, of spirit born!
Drink deeply, of His spirit here:
　　Nor let your heart be faint:
And you shall at the fount appear,
　　In heaven, a lovely saint!
Quite pure, and holy, right and just,
　　Made perfect while below:
Then, disembodied, from the dust;
　　To Jesus Christ you go!
Reclining, bask in beams of love!
　　And see Him, face to face:
In yon bright spirit world above,
　　The Author of free grace!
And as He is, so we shall be,
　　In body, soul, and spirit;
With whom to reign eternally,
　　And all His bliss inherit!

The Father, Son, and Holy Ghost,
  (The three, in spirit one:)
Likewise the splendid brilliant host;
  Millions before us gone!
Who, wait their kindred to receive,
  On yon, thrice happy shore!
Where those, who now in Christ believe;
  Shall meet, to part no more.
Loud hallelujahs, let us sing,
  To Christ, the Lamb of God:
Who did to us, salvation bring,
  And seal'd it with His blood!
A sigh, a groan, a briny tear,
  These are effective things;
Hope, love and joy, sad doubt and fear;
  Fly rapid on their wings!
With tidings brave, or mean, to those,
  For whom they each concern:
Creating friends, or bitter foes,
  Who may rejoice, or mourn.
Far distant they, or nigh at hand,
  Shall answer every call
Which spirits give, with full command,
  To bid you rise, or fall.
We cannot speak a single word,
  Or think one single thought;
But in the spirit world, 'tis heard;
  Nor can they pass for nought!
Conceiv'd, or utter'd, off they fly,
  Into the ambient air;
As lightning quick, but never die;
  Spirits, are everywhere!

Th' effects of which, are felt and seen,
    By all the human race :
And ride majestic currenteen ;
    In colours on the face !
An evil spirit, wanders far ;
    Seeking a place of rest :
But like an ill foreboding star,
    Which never can be blest !
The base design'd, she meets with pleasure ;
    Who, hand in hand go on :
To whom, she promises a treasure ;
    Till all they have, is gone !
The spirit world is wonderful !
    Of which, we each are one :
But what is man, of spirit null ?
    Perhaps you say he's gone !
Gone, sure enough ; but where, my friend ?
    This, you can hardly tell ;
We hope he did to heaven ascend,
    Where spirits all fare well ;
On this, or yon side of the grave,
    Where each and all appear ;
The sympathy you cannot waive,
    Connected far, and near.
Thoughts, words, and deeds, are all as one,
    For man to give account ;
Whereby the spirit's lost, or won
    Into, or from the fount !
" Father of Spirits," God of love !*
    Centre, and life of all :

* Hebrews xii. 9.

On earth beneath, and heaven above,
　The great, as well as small,
Whose equal privilege while here,
　Is, to obtain one thing :
Possess'd of which, you've nought to fear,
　In presence of the King !
To all the spirits, which have breathed,
　The Holy Ghost, on earth ;
Spiritual bodies are bequeathed,
　Of more than human worth.
This is the spirit world, my friends ;
　Beyond you cannot soar :
Just here, my vital subject ends ;
　And I, shall say no more !

———

BUY THE TRUTH, AND SELL IT NOT !

In lovely and instructive mood,
　I now incline to give,
Some pleasing sentimental food,
　To such, as wish to live.
Not in voluptuous dissipation,
　But seek a higher state,
Than they, who look for exaltation,
　From the ignobly great.
Fair truth, the fool will only bite,
　Nor by it can be blest :
For he hath got no appetite,
　Or stomach, to digest.

While in the Garden you are found,
　　Culling the best of fruit;
You wouldn't gather the unsound,
　　But cast it to the brute!
By this example, serve the mind,
　　With all superior juice:
And throw vulgarity behind,
　　But store the truth, for use.
Then, let the trees be good and fair,
　　From which you gather fruit:
To thrive, beneath the dresser's care,
　　Nor dirty hands pollute.
Sweet Nature's voice, is ever heard,
　　In one harmonic strain;
To speak the truth, in deed, and word;
　　Which never genders pain.
Let books, or conversation, and
　　The company you keep;
Be such, as honest truth command,
　　From which, you virtue reap.
I speak in terms that you may try,
　　What sages understood;
The truth in toto, you must buy;
　　Nor sell, the mental food!

Q

PATHOSITY; NAOMI AND RUTH.

Two Ephrathites dwelt, with their parents at Moab,
   From Bethlehem Juda they came ;
And each took a wife, with the virtuous robe,
   Which Ruth wore, of eminent fame !
As Elimeleck and his sons, were soon dead,
   The mother and daughters were left,
Poor widows indeed, who must seek their own bread,
   For each, is of husband bereft !
Naomi then, said to her daughters-in-law,
   " Return to your mothers again ;
And the Lord deal kindly to you, if ye go
   Your journey may not be in vain."
She kindly in sympathy, kiss'd them and wept ;
   Each damsel did bitterly cry ;
But Ruth to her bosom had tenderly crept,
   Saying, " leave you, dear mother ! not I,
Pray don't thus entreat me again for to leave
   A parent, the choice of my heart ;
Tho' God in his providence me did bereave,
   Death only, shall cause us to part.
And whither thou goest, for certain I'll go ;
   Wherever thou lodgest, I'll lodge ;
Then, no more solicit, or trouble me so,
   From thee, my departure to urge.
Thy kindred, my people for ever shall be ;
   Thy God, is the God I adore :

Whose grace is sufficient to give liberty,
 Or unite us, as heretofore."
Naomi, and Ruth, now to Bethlehem went,
 In harvest, expressly to glean ;
Tho' Ruth had in prospect another intent,
 Where faith, hope, and virtue are seen !
In the field of Boaz, she happen'd to land,
 He look'd on the damsel, so fair :
And said to the reapers, " let fall from your hand,
 Some corn, and she'll gather it there !"
But mark the salute, when he came to the field !
 Imploring " the Lord be with you ;"
The reapers retorted the blessing, unseal'd,
 Pronouncing the same on him, too.
Full liberty, freely was granted to Ruth,
 Who labor'd from morning to night ;
Likewise in the house, with his maidens forsooth,
 He'd have her to stay, within sight.
Then he gave the men charge, to treat her so kind,
 That nothing her person molest :
He saw the fair damsel, of excellent mind,
 With whom before long, he was blest.
" The Lord God of Israel, grant you reward ;
 And recompense thee, for thy care,
Dear Ruth ; I have heard, that thy fortune was hard,
 But come to me ; fare as I fare !
Beneath the bright wings of Jehovah to trust,
 By wisdom alone thou art led ;
And this is the version, confess it I must :
 Emanuel ! Jesus the head !"
Then she fell on her face, and bow'd to the ground ;
 To grateful expressions gave vent :

And this is the proof, that His favour she found,
   Whose smile, is the key of content!
Tho' death may dissever us here, for awhile;
   From whom, we are sorry to part:
Yet those who survive, may in sympathy smile,
   If still they have union, at heart.
Hence, Ruth dwelt at peace, with her mother-in-law,
   And labour'd all day in the field;
Then brought the proceeds to Naomi, who saw
   The gleans, made a beautiful yield!
Quite astonish'd to see the quantum of corn,
   For use, in the cottage to lay:
Suspecting that some of it, must have been shorn;
   Said, " where hast thou gleaned to day?"
To her mother-in-law, she opened the truth,
   Who found that they all were akin:
Then she laid out her plans, in favour of Ruth;
   Some closer alliance to win.
Thus 'cute was the head of Naomi indeed,
   To which her kind daughter complied;
Where faith and hope join'd in the prospect of seed,
   That nothing on earth could divide!
The father of Jesse, was soon made her son,
   By Boaz, her husband and friend:
The line thus extended, in wisdom went on,
   Till Jesus, sprang forth in the end!
By whom, all the nations on earth shall be blest!
   The Harvest of reaping will come:
And we shall be found with the faithful at rest;
   Naomi, and Ruth, are at home!

THE SECOND COMING OF CHRIST.

THE END OF WAR, WITH UNIVERSAL PEACE.

THE things which shortly must be done,*
  Belong to you and me:
The battle, must be lost or won;
  On this side of the sea!
Which bounds in front the isthmus, of
  The two extremes of time:
The end of which, is far above
  My musicalic chime.
I daren't presume to soar beyond,
  What God reveals to man:
From whom, His secrets now are bound,
  In wisdom's golden plan!
Tho' in prophetic language, we
  May touch the lyric strings;
The end of time, we cannot see;
  Nor what to-morrow brings!
The mythy paths of bygone days,
  Are in the ocean lost:
Nor can we on the future gaze,
  Except, at present cost.
Those instruments, were never made;
  God's secret ways to find:
Tho' some, we see, in retrograde;
  To future, we are blind!

* Revelations xxii. 6.

2 Q

The Gospel light, shines bright and clear,
  Where knowledge must obtain :
Yet, wisdom only grants us here
  The loss of all, for gain !
The deep mysterious ways of God,
  Are past our finding out !
He, for a blessing, takes the rod,
  To drive off, fear and doubt.
That we by faith in Him may live,
  And always ready stand :
Waiting for all He hath to give,
  Who doth the world command !
The first appearance of our Lord,
  In mercy, was foretold :
By which, the Gospel voice was heard,
  In dreary days of old !
Tho' now, by Him, the light doth shine ;
  Yet we, are in the dark !
Respecting future ; (not divine,)
  Touching the Vital Spark !
Christ's second coming,* (when and where,)
  From us, is wisely hid :
Altho' we hope to meet Him there,
  As our forefathers did.
But, only at the trumpet's sound ;
  When Gabriel gives the call ;
The dead shall rise from under ground ;
  And then, shall Babel fall !
In grandeur, and majestic style ;
  (As never seen before,)

* Matthew xxiv. 36.

Jesus, the Lamb of God, shall smile,
  On all His precious store !
Ten thousand angels, bright and fair,
  Shall then attend their King !
Whom saints shall meet, and in the air,
  Sweet hallelujahs sing !
Ah ! then the grand symphonic strain,
  By eurythmatic tongues :
Shall welcome Christ's eternal reign :
  To whom, all heaven belongs !

THE OLD MAN'S BENEFIT, AND THE YOUTH'S PRIVILEGE; A WELL SPENT LIFE.

How happy is he, in the sunset of life ;
  Who has left all his troubles behind !
Far enough blown away, in the whirlwind of strife,
  Nor ever a pest to the mind.
Having quitted the whole, by surmounting the same,
  In the long catalogue of his years :
Nor occasion hath given, to tarnish his name,
  Or extract a big fountain of tears.
The mind is at rest, in a happy survey,
  Of days never squander'd or lost !
He bought up the fragments, while passing away ;
  Retaining the whole to the last !
His youth has been spent, in providing a store
  Of good things, to use in mid-life ;

Which, when the time came, did assist him the more,
　　To quash all the risings of strife.
On the years gone by, he can look back and see,
　　How Providence help'd him along ;
Whose hand (when in troubles,) did set him quite free,
　　To sing his Deliverer's song !
Rejoicing he travels, from morning to noon,
　　And having arriv'd at mid-day ;
Can never regret, its appearance so soon,
　　Nor tax it, with any delay.
Tho', while in the midst of his throng he can see,
　　The Alps of mid-life to arise :
Which would threaten to daunt, or spoil him his glee:
　　But, he has the hand that supplies !
Resolution and courage, with grace in the heart ;
　　No matter whatever betide :
Perseverance in duty, and with a fair start ;
　　O'er mountainous hillocks you ride !
Then, the down-hill of life, he can travel with ease,
　　And rest at his leisure awhile :
Regaling himself, in the westerly breeze,
　　To waft him along with a smile !
Behold him there sat, on his chair by the fire :
　　In the winter of age you may see,
The snowy white locks, on the head of the sire ;
　　A crown, to the happy and free !
In the sunset of life, he's blithe as the lark ;
　　That sings in the morning of day :
His lamp being trimm'd, he is not in the dark ;
　　But ready, to tow'r away !
To the mansions of bliss, and far from all sin,
　　With prospect that baffles compare ;

What an envious state, (you perceive,) to be in !
  Ah ! wouldn't you like, to be there ?
A convoy of angels, are ready at hand,
  Awaiting his spirit to greet :
And take the soul fitted, to yon happy land ;
  Where all his best friends he shall meet.
The Lamb that was slain, he shall see, face to face ;
  With whom, he held converse in prayer :
Whose glory, and dignity, brightens the place :
  And wouldn't you like to be there ?
His sun is now setting, where daylight appears,
  Resplendent, with prospect so fair :
Which never can end, in the rolling of years !
  Ah ! wouldn't you wish to be there ?
Then begin while in youth, and attend to the truth ;
  This picture is drawn for your sake :
That like the old man, you may strive while you can ;
  And with him the benefit take.

THE ROCK THAT IS HIGHER THAN I.*

LEAD me to the Rock, that is higher than I ;
  A mansion to build, that will stand
The wreck of all ages, and Satan defy,
  With his army, by sea or by land.
The wind, and the tide, and the raging of fire,
  In th' grand termination of time :

* Psalm lxi. 2.

When the elements melt, 'tis all I desire,
   To stand on the mountain, sublime!
Lead me to the Rock, that is higher than I;
   Outriding the storms of the vale:
Inundated with floods, that swell to the sky,
   And mount on the wings of the gale!
Yet, far above all, is the dignified Tower;
   And far beneath all, is its base:
Nor millions of armies, the standard can lower,
   Well founded in permanent grace.
Lead me to the Rock, that is higher than I,
   The rock, that will never remove:
Whose 'butments are truth, with a jointer, to tie
   All th' parties, secure in love!
The Rock of all Ages, Christ Jesus the Lamb,
   To whom the whole world can apply;
Is He, who was smit, by the noble I AM:
   The Rock, that is higher than I!
Hide me in its cleft, when the storms shall arise,
   Which cause me to sicken and die;
This is all I desire, that excellent prize:
   The Rock that is higher than I!

ILLUSTRATIONS OF GLORY, IN HEAVENLY VISION.

In sweet aspirations of mental delight,
   And heart overflowing with love,
My soul is uplifted, to scenery bright;
   From which I would never remove.

The vision's enchanting, and nobly sublime,
   In the midst of the rapt'rous gaze :
Surpassing all thought, in the bound'ries of time,
   Reveal'd by the " Ancient of Days !"
The bright Crystal Palace, of Angels and God,
   The streets that are paved with gold ;
And the fruits of the buddings of Aaron's bright rod :
   Are elegant things to behold !
Come hither, said one, I'll exhibit the scene,
   Which never was open'd before ;
Where the fields, are all clad, in sweet living green,
   The Shepherd, will open the door !
Never was there a scene, so delightfully fair,
   So pleasing, so healthful, and grand :
Here, saints are all breathing, the sweet balmy air ;
   Which floats in the bright happy land !
Where, the Mother of Nations, alone is the Queen ;
   And the Prince of the Universe, King !
The River of Life, in the midst to be seen,
   From whence the whole progeny spring.
The children of whom, as the bright stars of heaven,
   For ever and ever will shine :
A crown, and a sceptre, to each one is given ;
   But Jesus ! the glory be thine !
What more we shall have, in our privilege there ;
   The angels above cannot tell :
Sweet visions transcendant, the family share,
   In the land, where the holy, fare well !

A CHALLENGE TO SCRIBE WARRIORS.

CHALLENGE all the bards on earth,
　Who advocate fell war :
To bring their strong artill'ry forth ;
　And drive the demon's car !
Whose luciferic hellish glare,
　May startle timid folk :
And kindle rancour every where,
　Which ends in fire and smoke.
And nothing less, I must contend,
　Or better, can ensue ;
As all the evil passions blend,
　In one satanic clue.
But God, with might and majesty ;
　Omnipotence, and power !
Will cast them in the raging sea :
　And all their host devour !

MORAL.

The pen is my sword, in the spirit of truth :
　By the word of whose power divine !
Shall conquer the world, and the devil forsooth :
　Then Jesus : the glory is thine !

EXTRAORDINARY!

An Epicedium on hearing a Sermon by The Rev. Dr. Ryan, Beverley, from Genesis xxv. 8. July 18th, 1858, on the death of George Dale, of that place, aged 91 years.

OUR brother, hath finish'd his pilgrimage here,
    And landed in Canaan above ;
Where all the true hearted, in faith shall appear,
    And bathe in the fountain of love !
I saw him, when leaving the tent where he dwelt,
    In the wilderness, Ninety-one years :
Perturbed emotions, bespoke what he felt,
    While his eyes were suffus'd in tears.
Yet, the hope he retain'd within, was the buoy ;
    That lifted his spirit on high :
By faith in Christ Jesus, with triumph and joy ;
    He exclaim'd, " I'm ready to die !
I have fought the good fight, I've finish'd my course ;
    Henceforth there is laid up for me :
A crown of bright glory, in heaven, the source,
    From whence, is the high dignity !
Sweet Jesus is waiting, my soul to receive
    To himself, who bids the child come ;
For all things are ready, to those that believe,
    Dear sir, I am just going home !
Farewell, Brother Ryan, (my pastor and guide,)
    Thirteen years of Sabbaths, I've spent,
In time, with the flow, and the ebb of the tide,
    And now to depart, I'm content."

R

Exemplary character, certainly such
    As seldom we hear of, or see :
Nine years of good sabbaths, he sat in the church ;
    And never but once, absentee !
An old man he was, and quite full of years,
    As Abram, he gave up the ghost :
Having cast to the winds, his doubts and his fears,
    And join'd with the heavenly host !
The shock of ripe corn, was all ready to reap,
    And sever away, from the clod :
The chaff is blown off, and the grain will now keep
    Secure, in the garner of God !
He has enter'd upon, the sabbath of rest,
    From labour and turmoil, to cease :
With the God of his fathers, eternally blest ;
    The end of the just man, is peace !

A SUBLIME ADDRESS TO THE CHRISTIAN SOUL.

RISE my soul, arise ; superior to the trinkets, and the meagre toys of time and sense : nor with those trifling, transient, sublunary joys, demean thyself, beneath the dignity of man. Maintain thy rank and station, held supreme of earthly grandeur ! and thou shalt live, to see her shadows fly as feathers with the wind, or scatter'd far and wide, as atoms in the air ; commingl'd with the dust ! while in the desolating blast, is carried off the baneful jargon of discordant song ; and all the base effluvia rising thence. When every jarring string shall break, upon the rock of solid truth : while in the vortex of despair is hurl'd, all rancour, discord, and contention, to the fiendish source from whence they sprang. Then shalt thou soar, on virtue's silvery wings, high as the spangl'd firmament of heaven! yea, far beyond yon canopy above! where moons shall wax, to wane no more ; and brilliant stars magnificently grand, shall stud the azure sky! while suns immortal rise, and shine in one perpetual spring ; deck'd in their Maker's robe! marching in one progressive train, never to set again!—and all conspire to raise the harmony of heaven. Far surpassing bliss, which mortals can conceive, or angels ever grasp, with intellect sublime! And shalt thou, oh my soul! there join the vast create, and uncreated beings : 'mid the highest orders of intelligence divine! around the throne of Deity? to stand in file, or rank, where myriads more shall be ; whom Christ redeem'd from every ill. And nothing now remains for such, but real happiness in Him, the object of all praise, and endless adoration. Jesus, is the door ; on which the bright elastic hinges work ; secur'd alone by him, (the Golden Screw,) which all the powers of earth, and heaven ; can ne'er remove! And thus, admittance thou shalt gain, within the pearly gates of that most splendid, superb, Cyrstal Palace ; the seat of angels ; and of God! This great salvation now is free ; for all the vast posterity of Adam : whose more than pristine beauty, we behold in concert with the blest ; and gaze transported at the sight ; in sweetest hallelujahs sing the song of Moses and the Lamb! Then art thou, (oh my soul!) divinely lost ; in wonder, love, and praise!!!! Sing on, my heavenly muse!

GENERAL HAVELOCK'S QUERY.
(AN ANSWER IS REQUESTED.)

WOULD man from battle just emerg'd, and on the verge of an eternal world, call up his darling son to see, and then engage, (or enter on) the sad destructive game wherein he caught his final blow? And would the christian soul exclaim, ah! that my son was here, to witness all the bravery of his father, now upon the point of death! and see the desolating blast of powder, shot, and fire; the sword to cut and slay; the loud, and boldly fierce, tremendous cannon roar to hear! Likewise to see the fruit of these, in desolation lay: bodies by thousands welt'ring in their blood! the cries of murder, peal throughout the battle field. Humanity is surely lost, and grace, cannot be found. Methinks a christian Havelock never could desire, much less impose the dire destructive practice, on his much beloved son: who, at his first attempt to imitate example left, a victim soon may fall! as did his predecessor. Man the noblest work of God! was never made to murder, cut, and slay, his fellow man! In sympathy let reason speak, and gospel grace confirm the Truth which Britons do profess! Here would I dip my pen, in Jesu's crimson ink; and bring it from the fount, to prove, that he! hath died, that they might live! The Golden Rule likewise, he wrote and taught, that all might live in peace, and love! Example grand: with precept most sublime!

When panegyrics loudly sound,
  I wish to know their rise:

And whether bas'd on solid ground;
   The foolish, or the wise.
The vulgar, vague, and vastly queer;
   May build upon the sand :
And lay their 'butments insincere,
   Tho', truth alone, will stand.
When jostling elements engage,
   In one tremendous gust :
The Fabric tow'rs above their rage ;
   Firm, steady, true, and just.

HAVELOCK'S LAST WILL AND TESTAMENT: PROVED.

> " O sons of earth ! attempt ye still to rise
> By mountains piled on mountains, to the skies?
> Heav'n still with laughter the vain toil surveys,
> And buries madmen in the heaps they raise.
> Who wickedly is wise, or madly brave,
> Is but the more a fool, or more a knave."
>
> Pope's Essay on Man.

A CHRISTIAN Havelock, never could
   With his expiring breath ;
Call forth his son, to witness blood,
   And put mankind to death.
Contrary to the Gospel plan,
   Which Jesus Christ hath taught;
That man be merciful to man,*
   For whom, he pardon bought !

* Luke iii. 14.

2 B

" My son, obey your father's word,
 And vend satanic ire :
Take hold of blunderbuss, and sword ;
 At my command, give fire !
Drive off the Sepoys, cut and slay,
 The heathen nations all :
Then shall you win a glorious day !
 And make the rebels fall."
Surely the captain, (good and wise,)
 Could never utter this :
To gain (on earth,) a transient prize ;*
 And lose eternal bliss !†
His last good-will and testament,
 He, publish'd to mankind :
That all might see the way he went,
 And what he left behind.
Perhaps you say, the Hero bold ;
 Was honourably brave !
Nor would he ever quit his hold,
 Till sunk into the grave.
Thus, by example did he leave
 A legacy for John :
Trusting he would the same receive,
 And put his armour on ?
A patriotic grand display,
 Of valiance nobly given :
To shew that Havelock's won the **day**,
 And landed safe in heaven !
This parody, you know is true ;
 The statement too, is just :

* Habakkuk ii. 9. † Matthew v. 9.

And he shall reap his wages, due ;
Tho' dust return to dust !

THE EXAMINER.

Lecture on General Havelock, by The Rev. A. Mursell ; which
was delivered in the Wesleyan Centenary Chapel, Manchester,
and appeared in the "Scarbro' Mercury," June 19th, 1858
from which this Poem was suggested.

Tho' Kings, and Nobles, me deride ;
    And deprecate the muse :
The Prince of Peace, is on my side !
    Whose pen I humbly use.
If war is good, so racing must,
    And every other game :
Some Dukes and Lords, in gambling trust,
    To dignify their name !
Licentious habits have the great,
    And noble of the land !
Whereby to win the large estate,
    And held the chief command ?
Ambition, pomp, and low design,
    Their every action prove ;
Nor sentiment at all divine,
    The evil to remove.
And lower gents will patronize,
    Those men of high degree :
Who think themselves so wondrous wise,
    Commanding land and sea !

We read that war began in heaven !
　　But did it there remain :
The harmony of which to leaven,
　　And fix a deadly stain ?
Ah, no : the warriors soon were hurl'd
　　Into the burning lake :
Or sent into the nether world,
　　Their fill of war to take.
Where, base examples of the same,
　　Are set, in grand array !
And Noblemen, will play the game ;
　　Hoping to win the day.
Those, take the devil at his word,
　　Who, fill'd with vengeful ire :
Have cannon, blunderbuss, and sword,
　　At his command, give fire !
Thus, kill, and slay, or cut, and wound,
　　The mother's darling son ;
Or have him fast, in fetters bound,
　　And this they call, grand fun !
Those blund'ring folk, take trim for tram,
　　Mistaking dark for light ;
The wolf they seek, but slay the lamb :
　　And blow its brains outright !
Where law protects, for public weal,
　　Some think, that war is good :
But tell me, (if your heart can feel,)
　　Who spilt your father's blood ?
Plund'ring and pilf'ring is the game,
　　In which the vile delight ;
Whereby to gain a victor's name,
　　And call it, honour bright !

In which, humanity is lost:
Where, is the spark of grace?
Are both into the battle toss'd?
Quite foreign to their place.
But can the christian thus engage?
Can he the war defend?
Or join with luciferic rage,
Where peace, and comfort end?
Ah, no! he can't, nor will he fight
With carnal weapons, mark!
Within his breast he has the light,
Which dissipates the dark.
The Duke of Wellington knew well,
That christians have no right,
Within the battle field to dwell;
Or with each other fight.
" No business have they," said the Duke
" Within the army here:
Tho' sanction'd in the Pentateuch,
The Gospel now shines clear!
Those men of mind, with notions nice,
In battle won't be seen;
Where vicious habits foster vice,
And every action mean!"
Tho', in the dark, and gloomy age,
When kings had truth in trust:
Fell passions rose with furious rage,
For not one man, was just!*
The Gospel day, unlocks the truth,
To those who will agree!

* Psalms liii. 3.

And hear the joyful call (forsooth,)
  To peace, by land and sea !
Without the sword or blunderbuss ;
  Our battles must be won :
And they who strive to conquer thus,
  Will find their work, well done !
The battle is not to the strong,
  Who think themselves, all might :
Vengeance and justice do belong
  To God, who judges right !
Peace, and good will, on earth, to **man** ;
  The Saviour came to bring :
Tho', mortals, counter to him ran ;
  And flapp'd their murky wing !
Saints, wrestle not with flesh and **blood** ;
  But, with satanic power :
By weapons, spiritual and good ;
  Upon the highest tower !
Wherewith, if we but use them right,
  Are sure, all rage to quell :
Through Christ alone, whose love and **might**,
  Conquer'd, both earth and hell !
The potsherds of the earth may fight,
  And each contend with other :
But can the christian think it right,
  To kill, and slay his brother ?
See, in the house of God forsooth,
  (A consecrated place :
Where Ministers of Christ, in truth
  Contend for peace and grace,)
A Rev. Mursell, mounted high
  Extenuating war :

By sentiments he can't supply
  In Christ, the Morning Star!
The unregen'rate man, may strive,
  And do the devil's will:
But men with grace and truth alive,
  The Gospel laws fulfil,
An Havelock's brave, heroic fame,
  Is spread from sea to sea:
With credit to his honour'd name,
  Who strove for victory.
Tho', when a youth, with courage bold,
  And carnal passions strong:
Himself into the army sold,
  To battle, right or wrong.
But, when reflection caught his mind,
  In retrospective view;
He saw, the practice was unkind;
  And half began to rue.
The light of grace shone on his heart,
  Said he, " Dear Lord, I'm fast:
With all my sins, I fain would part;
  Ah! save my soul at last!
Canst thou not in the battle field,
  Favour on me bestow?
Myself to thy good cause I'll yield,
  And fight for thee below."
Thus, bold and valiant Havelock rose,
  (At Lucknow, see him there!)
Before he went against the foes,
  His army's all at prayer!
This seems a wond'rous thing to scan,
  But, let the Prince have grace:

Wherewith to do the best he can,
   He's right, in every place.
As such, the prayer was heard no doubt,
   A chosen vessel he :
Engag'd to drive the devil out,
   And chase his progeny !
Peacemakers, are pronounced blest ;
   By Christ, the Prince of Peace :
Who came to comfort the distrest,
   And cause sad war to cease.
Mark, the ear of Malchus, which was smote,
   And sever'd by the sword :
Jesus, a miracle then wrought,
   And heal'd him, by His word !
" Put up thy sword again," said He,
   " For they who use the same ;
Shall perish by it, and shall be,
   Consum'd amid the flame !
Disputest thou my Father's skill,
   Omnipotence, and grace ?
Commanding legions, at His will,
   The enemy to chase !"
Then, let all christians trust in Him,
   And cursed war shall cease :
This is the lamp we have to trim,
   Which shines in gospel peace !
Be not deceiv'd, nor mock your God !
   For as you sow, you reap :
Vengeance, is the Almighty's rod,
   To make the rebels weep.
Heathens, and Christians, all were made
   By Him, who will command :

Nor suffer truth to retrograde,
 Justice, is in His hand !
When Herod's bold oration, gave
 Impetus to the flame
Of passion, burning nigh the grave,
 Wherein he sank with shame :
And in the midst of haughty pride,
 Was eaten up of worms !
While yet alive, and then he died,
 Scripture this truth affirms.
For arrogated praise of man,
 A judgment thus is given :
That we may learn the honest plan,
 To praise the God of heaven !
Let panegyrics on the war,
 And mortal warriors cease :
Nor adulate the Morning Star,
 The great grand Prince of Peace !

SOBRIETY, WITH THE LITTLE BIRD IN HAND.

IN what state should we all be found,
 When nigh the hour of death ?
Which cannot then the conscience wound ;
 Or yet pollute the breath.   Sobriety.
In what state should we wish to go,
 And meet the Bridegroom now ?
The Judge of all the world below !
 And at His footstool bow.   Sobriety.

s

If you would reap the grand reward
   In truth and equity !
Maintain what never will retard,
   The same eternally.   Sobriety.
And then amid the host above,
   In yon thrice happy state !
Where all is joy, and peace, and love,
   You ne'er shall deprecate   Sobriety.
Let all rejoice they've not to buy,
   The thing of which I tell—
And you may guess the reason why,
   The Landlord cannot sell   Sobriety.
Agents the devil has to do,
   His drudgery on earth ;
Who pop their foot into the stew—
   And spoil the best of broth.   Sobriety.
Be sure you never taste their mess,
   Nor furnish them with spoon,
To stir about your own distress ;
   And waste the lovely boon,   Sobriety.
This subject, men of sense (who read)
   Will fully understand—
That they may have, in time of need ;
The little bird in hand, viz., The product of Sobriety.
What gives to man a dignity,
   Beyond his fellow man ?
(Who never knew benignity,
   But, counted as a ban,)   Sobriety.
What gives to man a master's head,
   Sufficient for his station ?
Whereby he makes his daily bread ;
   Nor heeds a proud relation.   Sobriety.

What is it causes man to vouch
　An honest independence?
With which he never need to crouch,
　Or bend, to mean attendants?　　Sobriety.
What is it, honesty promotes,
　Industry, truth, and love?
By him, who leisure time devotes,
　Intemp'rance to remove?　　Sobriety.
What is it brings in wealth and fame!
　To him, who strives with pleasure
Thus, to mantain a noble name
　By every legal measure?　　Sobriety.
What is it gives unto mankind,
　Determinative power;
Wherewith the enemy to bind:
　Who would all peace devour?　　Sobriety.
What most contributes to the weal
　And welfare of a nation?
(Whereon, be stamp'd the British seal!
　True mark of admiration!)　　Sobriety.
What is it makes the home so sweet!
　Which used reverse to be,
But now the house is clean, and neat,
　With all the inmates free?　　Sobriety.
What is it makes the children smile
　To see their father come,
And run to meet him, (half a mile,)
　To welcome him at home?　　Sobriety
What is it makes the wife rejoice!
　Anxious to do her best,
To please the object of her choice,
　And strive to make him blest?　　Sobriety.

What is it gives man time to think,
  And live the life design'd !
By Him, who form'd the marriage link
  With love, and joy, combin'd ?   Sobriety.
What is it grants the drunkard free
  Admission into grace !
Whereby he may rejoice, and see
  The smile of Jesu's face ?   Sobriety.
What was it, in the midst of which
  Appear'd so charming there—
When Paradise receiv'd her touch
  Of sweet, salubrious air ?   Sobriety.
In what state did the world appear
  When God pronounc'd it good ?
And water gave, (not mad'ning beer,)
  To drink, with wholesome food ? Sobriety.
With what did reason first unite
  The moral hemisphere ;
Which gives to man the polish bright,
  And shews him how to steer ? Sobriety.
What course is that in which he should
  Pursue his earthly way ?
And practise every moral good !
  If he, would win the day ? Sobriety.

MORAL.

As nothing less we must maintain,
  To bring the standard forth—
And prove, possession here, is gain :
  But there, of endless worth !

'Twas granted to us from above,
   Never to give or sell!
The product of its Author, " Love !"
   And always answers well—   Sobriety.

A DISSERTATION ON DEATH.

H Death! thou monster; styl'd terrific! what art thou in reality? tell me? or, I shall trace thine origin! when in chaotic form, thy body was without a soul! and still remains the same : thus, void of sensibility! nor pain, or pleasure ; grief, or joy ; could thee, or thine possess! Then, what art thou : but the grand annihilator of the senses. Our aches and pains, our sorrows and our griefs ; no more disturb this mortal frame, when thou appears! Then, where art thou terrific? is it in fancy, whim, or imbecility of mind? which sees the phantom, and construes it to a ghost, a bear, a monster, or a fiend, altho', it never saw a shadow more alarming than its own. And art thou called Death? Death be thy name ; thou cannot have a better : just opposite to life. And if to me, this life is but a burden : then, why should I repine, or grieve to lay it down? No hyperbolic language do I use; the truth I shall declare! A friend thou art indeed ; to those who make the best of life : securing thus, the golden mean ; whereby to enter (through thy medium) into life eternal! Then, why art thou terrific? and

2 s

whence thy awful name ? 'Twas sin, and sin alone, that made thy visage pale : and thus transferr'd the monstrous epithet on thee ! but, He who never sinn'd ; had innate power to change the King of Terrors ! (and did,) into a messenger of peace, whereby the Prince of Glory ! first made exit from this earth, to heaven.—And then, the passage way for us, was made secure.

And where's the monster now ? Oh Death ! where is thy sting ? The victory, through Christ alone, is ours ! Then, never let the christian soul despair of life ! tho' in the midst thereof we are in death : yet, 'tis a pleasing and delightful thought, that death, is but the passage to eternal life. Can we with Job then say ? " All the days of my appointed time will I wait till my change come !"* and with Paul : " For me to live is Christ ; to die is gain. Blessed are the dead which die in the Lord : yea, so saith the Spirit ; for they rest from their labours, and their works do follow them.

ON LIFE AND DEATH.

INTERLOCUTORY.

Oh Death : grim monster ! where is thine abode ? and where thy terror ? art thou in mind, or body ? if in the mind of man thy seat is taken, then his days are gloomy, and his nights terrific ! bordering on despair.

* Job xiv. 14.

But if in body only thou exist; then life, is life; and thou art but a shadow!—Hold, hold friend: allow me now, to answer for myself. My name is Death: a worthy messenger I am, to all corrupted things; which cannot bear, their own existence! Matter, must decay; and Death, is ready then; to grant it sweet release. But, suffering humanity alone, can find the true benignity of Death! Here, in man's bosom dwells a fear, far worse than Death itself: which sin created; and then was found the vile contaminated piece of earth, in which the spirit dwells, and both must surely die, but, for the restorator, whose messenger I am! to cut the mortal part in mercy down; and cast it in the tomb, to mingle with its native earth, from whence it first arose. And shall I then be call'd a monster, for the office I sustain? Remember all the ills of life, in which you live; the sickness and disease: together with the dark tempestuous sea! whereon ye sail! Then tell me, would you like to live in this most wretched state for ever? now come, speak the truth; would you? nay. you'd want an extricator: such am I! and nothing more, or less. Death you need, to rest your weary limbs; by age, or something else occasion'd.—Then where are all thy terrors Death? and where is thy grim face? thou makes it quite a beauty! a lovely, charming thing to be desir'd: as thus, necessity must own. But what art thou? I still demand an answer. Come, speak the truth a little farther, please.—With reverence I'll adhere! A name, a name terrific, in the mind of some, and that is all! Altho,' a messenger of mercy sent to all, in all, for all; that all may live, nor die the death that never dies! The passage only into life I am! to those alone through Christ prepar'd. One gentle touch of mine, and then the scene is chang'd! the soul shall quit its mortal tenement of clay! and drop it, mouldering in the dust: to lay and be refin'd, according to the mighty working of its Author! to be reviv'd again, but clear of sin, and death! yet, at the final scene: the soul takes wing, and flies away to its eternal rest; conducted by a splendid host of those who're gone before, to realms of light, and life, and love; in blissful day! "far from a world of grief and sin, with God eternally shut in!" Am I then, a friend; or enemy to man? come, speak the truth to me.—An enemy, 'tis said thou art, whatever thou may say: mankind will ever hold thee such. Man cringes at thy name!—Well, be it so; for that is all I am, and where I come, all life is fled; as I have none myself, or ever had. Death now, is swallow'd up of life, (in Christ,) and He is all, in all! Then, am I left an empty nought; bereft of every thing, name and all! with neither body, soul, nor spirit!—Well well, and that seems good enough for thee. But yet I want to know why thou art here at all; a pest; and frightful torment unto man!—The secret I'll divulge again, you seem to try my patience! A charge I have, a message unto all! (and must the same fulfil.) The rich, the poor, the high, the low, the great, the small, the wise man and the fool, the learned and unlearn'd: all, all without exception, must bend beneath my scythe! for I shall level all! and then, I've done.—It's high time, I think: for time with us will then be ended! Thou grim, shrewd, dark, thievish, cunning, and insidious monster! who, with the grave art nigh akin: you seem to swallow all, and never have enough! rapacious, gormandizing

pair, as ever had a name! And yet, oh Death: thou
says, thou'rt but a name! Pray how does this appear?
If so, thou never could be born: nor ever die!—That's
right, and goes to prove me naught but name: and no
deceiver. When first I made appearance in this world:
I came to rid it, of its rubage*; tho' you may think it
queer, yet I am right: a messenger of mercy still am I,
for that grand purpose! Perhaps you say, all good goes
with it: but I say no; the things which good and pious
are, I cannot touch!—Well, well; thou speaks like one
with sense and wit: altho', a name alone thou art.
'Tis said, that " Friendship's but a name, a charm that
lulls to sleep; a shade that follows wealth and fame,
but leaves the wretch to weep!" Methinks thou art in
truth, the better of the two. A friend art thou in need?
a friend indeed. If what thou says be true, and that
we can't disprove. But yet to ascertain, we all must
die! and this the living know. The seeds of which
are in our mortal system sown!—Right again thou art,
and this is mercy too, or else mankind would rarely
think, or strive to be prepar'd for my approach; whereby to meet the best of friends!—Well, well; grim
monster: the appellation yet is thine, to take it in the
gross; thou cannot be offended: a thing with name
alone! There is no wit, or knowledge in the grave, and
that's the spell for thee to use. We'll leave the matter
in the bud, that where its nature is, the fruit may grow,
and then, in death decay! Wild ruminations in the
head, the heart, or mind; cause us to die ten thousand
deaths before the proper time. More terrible than

* Matthew xiii.

thee : are they ! and when thou in reality appears ; they
all like shadows fly, and man begins to live !—Altho',
my name is Death : I must admit thou's spoken truth,
and truth will live, when nature dies, and Death, has
fled away ! A passage only to the tomb, am I ! and
then no more of me. So now, I bid you all farewell.—
" Death through Christ, is swallow'd up in victory !"

" How blest the chamber where the good man meets
        his fate !
Privileg'd beyond the common walk of virtuous life ;
Close on the verge of heaven !"

PRIVILEGE AND ORNAMENT.

FIRST AND LAST.

MAN void of privilege, is like
    A ship without a sail ;
A desert land without a dyke,
    And horse without a tail.
Where ornament with use are not,
    Or drink to quench the thirst ;
The handle is without a pot,
    And but a vessel lost !
Yet, privilege to man is given,
    In every shape and form ;
Yea, more than six days out of seven,
    To guard against a storm.

And if the benefit he prize,
　(Which none can do, and die ;)
Then shall he in his nature rise :
　And hark, to reason high !
If all the days we're doom'd to live
　On earth, were spent in toil ;
We shouldn't have one day to give
　Ourselves, to rest awhile.
Altho' my fellow-creatures may,
　Forget the truth I state ;
By losing one, cast six away,
　And fix their own ill fate.
Mark well the use and ornament,
　We have, of one in seven ;
Which never should be vainly spent,
　If we would get to heaven.
The Sabbath is the day of rest,
　Altho' created last ;
By Christ, 'tis made more highly blest :
　And now, it is the first !

BOLD SIMPLICITY.

A GEN'ROUS fierceness is allow'd,
　To dwell with innocence ;
Where pride is rais'd above the shroud,
　Which hides all vain pretence.
The noble mind with honest bent;
　Can never turn aside :

Or subjects falsely represent,
  When conscience is the guide!
A bold heroic turn you'll find,
  With simple brazen face;
Characterise the man of mind,
  Replete with truth and grace.
Tho' some fastidious in their choice,
  Will court a pleasing smile;
From those who have a charming voice,
  Hypocrisy and guile!
But let a friendly word be spoke,
  In rough, tho' ready wit;
The man of sense without a joke,
  In truth attends to it.
Some two fac'd gents there are who will
  Appear what they are not;
(The scripture statement to fulfil,)
  "Are neither cold, nor hot."
Let truth and honest dealing be,
  Your motto and your theme;
In every line of conduct free,
  To merit all esteem.
A humble boldness then you have,
  With dignity of soul:
Which shall the conqueror's banner wave,
  While endless ages roll!

THE ORIGIN OF HUMANITY.

Humanity! thou heav'n born child:
   On man alone conferr'd,
When God on human nature smil'd,
   And all creation stirr'd.
While every living thing on earth,
   Was dust alone refin'd ;
Excepting man of higher birth,
   And he was bless'd with mind !
Whence, all good feelings that arise
   Within his honour'd breast ;
The dignity which never dies,
   But makes him truly blest !
When pity and compassion join,
   With mercy in display ;
Our brightest faculties combine,
   And chase midnight away.
Behold, the President divine !
   When chaos he beheld,
Who caus'd his sun thereon to shine,
   And darkness was dispell'd.
Then, bright benignity appear'd,
   Darting its rays on earth ;
By which creation's sons were cheer'd,
   And human laws had birth.
Thus, do to others, as you would
   Have others do to you ;
As if perchance you happen could,
   Just step into their shoe,

T

See and admire the gen'ral feast,
   Prepar'd for all that live !
The man, the reptile, and the beast,
   'Tis Godlike, thus to give!
Dumb creatures oft by signals speak,
   And mercy do implore,
Of those who never strive or seek,
   God's goodness to adore.
To sympathise with the distrest,
   Is man's prerogative ;
And make the brute creation blest,
   While under him they live.
Whose mortal origin is one,
   With all who breathe the air !
And when the vital breath is gone,
   Alike to dust repair.
Yet, reason, love, and dignity ;
   To man alone are given
With feelings of benignity,
   Whose origin is heaven.

THE ORIGIN OF PRINCIPLE.

oOD principle was first instill'd,
   Within the human breast ;
Likewise the sentiment fulfill'd,
   That man is truly blest.
The humane feeling is divine,
   Its origin was such :

And man, did as his Maker shine,
   Who bore his Author's touch.
Whose stamp and signature remain,
   On his high honour'd brow :
By which the life eternal gain,
   And Christ shall tell us how.
Perversity on vileness bent,
   With own self-will and way ;
Let in a stream of discontent,
   And we all, ran astray !
As sheep without a shepherd then,
   Yet Jesus undertook
Our cause, and brought us back again,
   As home, we had forsook.
Compassion thus made manifest,
   In its divinest form ;
Determin'd man should still be blest,
   Altho' a sinful worm.
" Come unto me," the Saviour said,
   " And I will thee restore !
My blood was for thy ransom shed,
   Thy burden, I have bore ! "
Altho' humanity was lost,
   And every blessed thing ;
All are restored, at the cost,
   Of Jesus Christ our King !

REVELATIONS BY AUTHORITY.*

And is the talent to compose,
    A few short verses, given
To one who shall the truth disclose,
    Secrets reveal'd in heaven?
In virtue of His honour'd name,
    Whose wisdom hath no bound;
Altho' His dignity and fame,
    Are spread the world around.
Yet is the truth in grand display,
    Reveal'd in partial strains;
Increasing to the perfect day,
    Long as himself remains!
The hidden secrets of the Lord,
    Are in His bosom bound;
Where future blessings now are stor'd,
    For those who grace have found.
And when the day-spring from on high,
    In splendour doth appear;
Then shall the armies of the sky,
    Announce their Captain near.
Whose second visit to our world,
    In majesty and power;
Shall prove the secrets then unfurl'd,
    In that momentous hour!
But what am I now speaking of?
    Where is the Book unseal'd?
And where the message from above?
    Whence are the truths reveal'd?

* I Corinthians xii.

Mark, in comparison of which,
    Sweet music is discord ;
The major, or the minor pitch,
    Can not the whole afford.
But, I'll unriddle this to those,
    Who apprehend my theme ;
" The best of Author's can't compose,
    To merit all esteem."
Nor can the finite comprehend,
    Or grasp infinitude ;
Altho' he sit beside his "Friend :
    Who fed the multitude : "
Then listen to the voice of truth ;
    " Attend the gospel sound ; "
Glad tidings are to all forsooth,
    And all, the truth have found.

THE MERIDIAN SPLENDOUR.

'Twas on the sweet morn, of last midsummer day ;
    When all things, were lovely an' grand :
I sat in the garden, so pleasing and gay,
    Where sweets, by the zephyrs were fann'd.
While mountains, and vallies, were clad in costume,
    All lovely and fair to behold !
Diffusing their odours, in splendid perfume,
    And flow'rs were tinged with gold !
The Queen of the Morning was hailing the Sun,
    And sang the melodious tune !
    2 T

Which Shepherds delight in, when Spring hath put on
  Its dress, for the middle of June.
Behold now, and hearken to nature around !
  While all the wee songsters unite,
In the musical song, with harmonic sound,
  On the day which hasn't a night.
Then see the green leaf, on the plant, and the flower,
  Of every tincture and hue :
On which the rain drops, in a genial shower,
  Or otherwise, falling as dew.
But look at the fruits of the earth from the bud,
  Maturing, for us to partake !
Who, once were like them, when pronounc'd very good :
  And nothing was made by mistake.
Allow me to draw out your minds farther still,
  And gaze on the animal race ;
Who, by instinct are led, not needing a will
  To fix either purpose or place.
None accountable those, so active and gay
  Passing time to gratify sense ;
Nor apprehend danger, they gambol and play,
  But never with guile or pretence.
Brave man as a potentate, rides in the air !
  Or walks in the midsummer breeze !
When mind is devoid of all trouble and care,
  The picture before him will please.
All things at his pleasure, nor aught to control
  The man, under reason and grace ;
He may take what he needs, of the sweets in the bowl,
  But never himself to displace.
Each shade in the mirror, I place to your view,
  A certain position requires ;

Wherein you may see all created anew,
 Which none but the christian admires.
The midsummer's day, or the mid-stage of man ;
 To which all attention be given :
Is drawn out upon the meridian plan,
 And gives you an aspect of heaven !
Examine it close, in the beautiful drift
 Of natural things, you perceive ;
For while all the seasons of life have their shift,
 They do but each other relieve.
A sketch of the beauty's in nature you see,
 Transfer the whole subject to mind ;
On a scroll that is pure, unspotted and free,
 And then the midsummer you find !
Yet autumn and winter come on in their place ;
 My meaning is, mortal decay :
No matter for that, they are ripening in grace,
 Who live, in meridian day !
Maturing for ever, till time pass away :
 And eternity burst on the view !
Then, then you behold the grand midsummer day,
 And everything formed anew !
Yes, sow the good seed, and in harvest you'll reap
 The fruit of your labour, (so grand ;)
When cross'd the high swellings of Jordan, you leap
 Direct to the fair promis'd land !
Sufficient is said, acting faith on the Lamb,
 That was slain, and revived again ;
With whom you shall be, th' immortal I AM !
 May His Holiness grant it.   Amen.

THE INTELLECTUAL PLANTATION.

This world's a nursery for the next,
　Where plants immortal grow;
Nor scrupling use the vain pretext,
　Disputing what we know.
Yet man will toil for matter hid,
　In base terraqueous stuff;
He'll screw to grasp what God's forbid,
　Nor ever gets enough.
The mind of whom, I must contend,
　Coeval is with time;
The weight of which will make him bend,
　Before he reach his prime.
The intellectual part of man,
　Its zenith can't attain;
Design'd infinitude to scan,
　While oceans yet remain.
A life's consummate happiness:
　A sea without a shore!
Can never neap, or yet grow less,
　Than is the boundless store!
Man's privilege, runs on apace!
　But tell me where it ends?
A period, never found its place,
　Where endless bliss extends.
Aspiring to infinitude,
　Nor ever reach the mark;
Tho' in sublimest altitude;
　Of Deity a spark!

To shine immortal as the sun,
   Transparent as the sea !
Which John in Patmos sally'd on,
   And sails eternally.   .
Enjoying all ! the vision's fled !
   Reality appears !
And saints have got the golden thread,
   To spin for endless years !
The wheel of time, will run its length,
   And matter drop away ;
But mind, shall then improve in strength,
   Nor ever feel decay.
While every heart is tuned to sing,
   The praises of the Lamb !
Their truly worthy Lord and King ;
   Jehovah, great I AM !
This privilege ! none can excel ;
   The half has not been told :
Nor ever shall, till all fare well ;
   And Jesus we behold !

THE FALL OF BABEL PROGNOSTICATED.

ALL time, and tide, and winds, obey
   A certain voice on high !
The sea, the land, the rippling spray,
   Can not the voice deny.
The tow'ring rocks in silence nod,
   Obeisance to His will ;

For each proclaim their Author, God!
  And must His work fulfil.
When boist'rous winds with fury blow,
  And wild commotions rise;
Vast nature seems to feel and know,
  The edict, by surprise!
Yet time progressive, hastens on
  The strange catastrophe;
Which all shall witness, as in one,
  Fix'd, from eternity!
The fall of Babel was decreed,
  By Him who rais'd the tower;
So prominent in Adam's seed,
  Which did its standard lower.
We, with alternate hope and fear,
  Behold it tott'ring now!
The fall of which, is happen near;
  I'll state the time, and how.—
When Gabriel shall in person, stand
  Upon the ocean shore;
And swear by Him, who holds command,
  That time shall be no more!
The elements a flaming void!
  The sun, the moon, and all
The twinkling stars, must be destroy'd;
  And thus, shall Babel fall!
No more to rise in grand display;
  No never, never more:
But mark, the superb splendid day
  Appears, with all its store!
Nothing terraqueous in the whole,
  Or crumbling matter then;

When Babel has obtain'd her fall,
  Never to rise again !
For time, and things, have pass'd away ;
  No more shall they return :
As all have nature's debt to pay,
  This lesson, each must learn.
However dull the scholar be
  He must attend the call,
And witness this catastrophe,
  Babel must surely fall !

THE CRUCIFIX.

Ah ! blessed Jesus ! who for me,
  Did pain and grief endure ;
And died upon th' accursed tree,
  Salvation to procure.

Gethsemane can witness yet,
  The agonising pain ;
Which caus'd big drops of bloody sweat,
  To issue from each vein !

The soldier's spear then pierc'd His side,
  While hung upon the tree,
Whereon he bled, and groan'd, and died,
  To set the captive free.

The dead were rais'd, the rocks were rent!
　In consternative fear;
All nature wept, in deep lament,
　His dying groans to hear!

The orient sun withdrew his light,
　Convulsions seiz'd the globe;
The planets then! (which shine so bright,)
　Put on their sable robe.

'Mid lightning's flash, and thunder's roar,
　The bold Centurion stood;
And cried, (as ne'er he did before :)
　" This is the Son of God !"

" 'Tis finish'd now," the Saviour said;
　Then bow'd his head and died!
For all, the precious blood is shed,
　Jesus! was crucified!

DESCRIPTIONS OF EARTH AND HEAVEN.

THE verdure of the landscape round,
　Is beauteous to behold;
Where flow'rs of varied hue abound,
　More precious far than gold!
The hawthorn and the woodbine now,
　Are edg'd with living green;
And health, sits smiling on the brow;
　Where Love, is nature's Queen.

Diffusing all her sweets around!
   Salubrious is the air,
Through which the birds of music sound,
   Their language everywhere.
So charming to the senses they,
   Delight the soul of man;
In splendid, unique, grand display!
   And odorif'rous fan.
Sweet breezes wafted by the same,
   With pleasure we inhale;
Far more than eloquence can name,
   Description all, must fail.
But ah! if mind is baffl'd in
   Describing what we see?
How then shall it with tongue begin,
   To trace Divinity?
Beyond the power of thought t' uprise,
   And shine in grand display!
Outstrips the genius of the wise,
   In every age, and day.
Yet man with privilege shall rise,
   To realms of high estate!
And soaring, mount the upper skies,
   Where love, can not abate.
This consolation here is given,
   That what we know not now;
Shall be reveal'd to all in heaven,
   Where scenes immortal grow!

U

THE PREMIER'S BENEDICTION.

Composed and sent to The Right Honourable Lord Palmerston,
by the Author, on Good Friday, 1857.

THANKS to you, my noble Lord,
   (Prime Minister of State !)
For peace and plenty now restor'd,
   By you, (to us, of late.)
As instrumental in the hand,
   Of Governor supreme ;
Who hath the nations at command,
   And merits all esteem !
The high position which you hold,
   Was by His wisdom given ;
In whose fair writings 'tis enroll'd,
   And ratified in heaven !
When monstrous tyranny prevail'd,
   In distant heathen lands :
Justice and mercy then assail'd,
   And bound the same, in bands,
Of christian love, and unity ;
   (Not with the tyrant's chain !)
That each and all may now agree,
   Never to fight again.
Nor ever, ever deviate,
   From honor, truth, and right ;
Then, shall we hold the best estate,
   Secure ; through Jesu's might.
Who did on this momentous day,
   The mighty conquest gain !

O'er sin, and death, our debt to pay ;
  That we might life obtain.
Hark ! how he cries while on the tree !
  Father ! I pray forgive :
Press all the burden upon me,
  But let the sinner live.
Ah ! may we each one, act our part ;
  Till from this earth we move :
To where the true sincere in heart,
  Shine forth in realms above !
Friend Palmerston, I trust to see,
  With all the good and great ;
Seated beside His Majesty,
  Who gain'd our lost estate !
God bless the Queen ! her consort too ;
  With all their progeny !
May every branch henceforward grow,
  A lovely fruitful tree !
And may our rulers, never swerve
  From rectitude, in power ;
But manifest the strongest nerve,
  On Britain's noble tower !
Where privilege and dignity !
  Are both in one combin'd,
With feelings of benignity,
  And love to all mankind !
Mark ! while we have a friend at helm,
  To guide the vessel right ;
That nothing may the same o'erwhelm,
  Each pull, with all their might !
Our work on earth, will soon be done,
  Our life, is but a span :

Yet, here the golden thread is spun,
 The privilege of man !
Enjoyment thus, in time have we,
 Likewise a future store ;
Reserv'd in heaven eternally,
 When time shall be no more.
Ah ! blessed state ! thrice blest indeed !
 Be this my ardent prayer ;
That each may now, in Christ succeed ;
 And claim a mansion there !

 * * * * *

I've little said, tho' much is meant ;
 The which, you apprehend :
With free goodwill, these lines are sent
 To our trustworthy friend.

THE GOLDEN STORE SECURED.

SILVER, and gold are His, who fills
 Immensity of space !
The cattle on a thousand hills,
 He owns, and points their place.
To every thing that breathes, he gives
 A portion of His store ;
And, without which, the world that lives,
 Would soon exist no more !
Mankind are not their own, and yet,
 A vast they occupy ;

Which none can either count or met',
   Between the earth, and sky !
And yet, a better store is given,
   Which must augmented be ;
To fit us for the bliss of heaven,
   And its sweet harmony.
Mark ! be our talent what it may,
   Of money, stock, or mind :
We must improve it, every day ;
   According to its kind.
And then our benefit is sure ;
   Nor can exhausted be :
The golden store, is made secure,
   To all eternity !

THE SPRING TIDE OF HUMAN LIFE.

THERE is a tide in man's affairs,
   (When taken at the flood ;)
Which lifts his bark o'er rocks, and bears
   Him on to something good.
But if he loiter, ebb succeeds,
   And leaves him clear and bare ;
The beach is cover'd o'er with weeds,
   And all for want of care.
Then, on a retrospective glance,
   He sees the spring-tide gone ;
And meand'ring cries, I've miss'd my chance :
   'Twill never more return !

2 u

As age and want, creep on apace,
    For which, did nought provide ;
These hoary locks, speak my disgrace,
    And prove the ebbing tide.
Vicissitudes in human life,
    Do both recede and flow ;
'Mid hope and joy, 'mid war and strife,
    We have to pull, and row :
While boist'rous winds, tremendous blow,
    And threaten to capsize,
Or sink the cargo down below,
    Where it can never rise.
Tho' waves are tossing to and fro,
    This little bark of mine ;
Yet, whence and whither bound I know,
    The sun, (tho' late,) may shine !
Thank God for that, the cheering thought,
    Springs up within my breast ;
That Jesus Christ salvation bought,
    To comfort the distrest.
Oh ! may I now fresh courage take,
    And muster all my strength ;
Through faith in Him, and for His sake,
    I'll gain the port at length !
Where storms and tempests rage no more,
    Mutations never come ;
On Canaan's lovely happy shore,
    Safe landed there ! at home.

COMMON SENSE.

THE man with good, tho' common sense,
　Will use the same and try,
His stock of knowledge to enhance ;
　And raise his station high.
Nor ever let vile passions mar,
　His judgment, sense and wit ;
Or else, they upset reason's car,
　And in her chair will sit.
To rule the man of common sense,
　The brute has got the power !
Who can with wisdom thus dispense,
　His dignity will lower.
Beneath the level of the beast ;
　The man is quite unman'd :
On carnal passions does he feast,
　Devoid of reason's wand.
If drinking habits he begin,
　The reel is turn'd about ;
Soon as base liquor enters in,
　Good common sense runs out.
Hereby, is vile infection spread,
　Which doctors cannot mend ;
And thus, the man is worse than dead,
　Without a single friend.

A MEMENTO

On the death of Father Wright, March 3rd, 1857, at his
Daughter's, Mary Siver, Bridgeport, Connecticut, America.

MARY, a favourite used to be ;
   And Father lov'd her well :
Witness, he cross'd the Atlantic Sea,
   With her at home to dwell.
And many happy days he spent
   (I trust,) along with thee ;
Enjoying peace, and true content ;
   Tho' far away from me.
Yet every day, my prayers have been,
   Sent up to heav'n for you ;
To practise nothing that is mean,
   But live as Christians do.
Sweet intercourse I've never had,
   With thee, since but a child ;
Excepting when my little lad,
   Look'd on his aunt, and smil'd.
'Tis four-and-twenty years gone,
   So rapid in their flight !
Since you address'd your brother John,
   And I, my sister Wright.
Never the scribble of a pen,
   Have you once sent to me ;
I've wonder'd ! o'er and o'er again,
   What can the matter be !

I trust, a brother's love remains :
   Sister's, you only know :
Yet, Father's blood runs through our veins,
   In sympathy to flow.
Such complicated feelings now,
   Pervade my throbbing heart ;
Nor can I, (sister,) tell you how ;
   Perhaps you feel the smart.
A good old age our Father saw,
   His years were Seventy-seven ;
And if but gone where christians go,
   He's landed safe in heaven !
Take courage then, and so prepare,
   To meet the sinner's friend ;
That you and I be with Him there,
   When mortal life shall end.

SUPPLEMENT.

Dear Father has gone, but I cannot tell where !
   His body, lays under the sod ;
And we in conclusion, shall thither repair ;
   To wait the appearance of God !
I trust he is happy ! and blest evermore ;
   Releas'd from the body of sin :
Through Christ, to enjoy the ineffable store !
   With those, who the victory win.

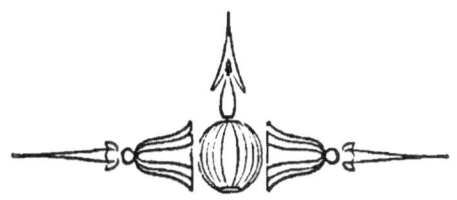

THE REGULATOR.

LET nothing too much you elate,
　And nothing depress you at all:
Extreme of the passions are great,
　And are sure to fling you a fall.

A mind that is easy and coy,
　And well regulated by grace;
Will fill you with comfort and joy,
　To move at a regular pace.

The time of the day you can tell,
　The day of eternity too;
Will sound as a musical bell,
　In every act, that ye do.

A time-piece, your body is here,
　Your soul, is the mainspring within;
Which musn't be ruled by fear,
　To drive away sorrow and sin.

But love, in your bosom will give,
　Impetus to every scheme!
Consisting of truth, while you live
　In harmony with the supreme.

And when your departure's at hand,
　A convoy of angels are sent;
T' convey you to yon happy land,
　Where all, are in peace and content.

'Mid friendship and amity sweet,
  Communion of saints, who above,
The song of redemption repeat,
  And bathe in the fountain of love!

For ever and ever to dwell,
  And bask in the beams of His face,
Who conquer'd the world, death and hell;
  By His own immaculate grace.

AN EPITAPH.

My body, lies in this grave-yard,
  Beneath the verdant sod;
My soul, hath gone to its reward,
  Lodg'd in the arms of God!
Who read this stanza, mark the end
  Of all your actions here!
Prepare in time to meet your Friend,
  And death, you needn't fear.

THE BACCHANALIAN POETS.

F tippling Poets spend in lush,
   What should be spent in meat;
They'll always be behind the bush,
   And seldom on their feet.
Such murd'rers ever are in need,
   While penning simple rhyme,
Will cut themselves until they bleed,
   And kill their precious time !
Of poverty they loudly sing,
   And curse their sorry fate ;
Because they feel its bitter sting,
   Who cannot love, but hate.
Their horrid practice I detest,
   Asham'd to call them brothers ;
Who (having means,) will not be blest,
   And tax the crime on others.
Such jinglers ought to stop their song,
   And never sing of evil ;
Who're agents of, and do belong,
   To Father Nickey, Devil !
This yelping discord is to me ;
   A dismal dreary sound ;
Destroying love and harmony,
   Where music should be found.

PARAPHRASE ON THE TWENTY-THIRD PSALM.

The Lord is my Shepherd! my comfort and guide;
 As I wander along in the vale:
Nothing good shall I lack, as he doth provide;
 Resources for me cannot fail.
On lovely green herbage, he gives me to feed,
 In pastures of pleasing delight:
All things are supplied, the most splendid indeed!
 While I keep in the path that is right.
Beside the still waters of comfort I stand,
 And view its perpetual stream:
Gliding on through the vale, at the shepherd's command;
 Who, the lambs of the flock, doth esteem!
Converted from sin, is the soul of the saint,
 In the pathway of holiness led;
By the hand of the Shepherd, who never can faint,
 Sustain'd by the water and bread!
Loving kindness, and mercy, shall follow me here;
 'Mid a world full of trouble and strife:
I'll dwell in the house of the Lord: (without fear,)
 In love, all the days of my life.
For ever and ever, and world without end,
 When pass'd through the valley below:
I still have my Shepherd! a wonderful Friend!
 To guide me, wherever I go.
Thus tranquil and happy, resigning my breath,
 While Jesus; hath hold of my hand:
I'll walk through the valley, and shadow of death;
 To the lovely, elysian land!

w

No ills shall I fear, for the staff and the rod,
   Of the Lord ; is the comforting bowl :
The smile of whose face, in the image of God !
   Reflecting the same on my soul !
Yea, I see, and I feel the oil, through the glass ;
   Anointing my eyes, and my head :
From glory to glory ! the flocks, shall then pass,
   Who, by the good Shepherd are led.

PRIVILEGE AT THE TABLE OF THE LORD.

(TUNE, TOM AND JERRY.)

SEE the table neatly spread !
       Come and welcome.
Jesus is the living bread !
       Come and welcome.
Take and eat, for He hath said,
       Come, and welcome.
Those who will on him be fed,
       Come, and welcome here.

Jacob's children, and his wife ;
       Live for ever !
Not in jarring, or in strife,
       Live for ever ;
But in praises, loud and rife,
       Live for ever :
All who taste the bread of life,
       Live for evermore !

Sweetest harmony is heard,
    So delightful!
When the Captain gives the word,
    So delightful!
By the trumpet of the Lord,
    So delightful!
Every harp is in accord:
    So delightfully.

Sounding praises, all divine!
    To His glory!
Suns immortal, then will shine,
    To His glory!
Am I in the living vine,
    To His glory?
Privilege is surely mine,
    To His glory now.

THE SATISFACTORY PORTION OBTAINED ON EARTH.

Can aught on earth, e'er satisfy
 Th' immortal part of man?
With all my ransom'd pow'rs, I'll try
 To find the golden plan!
Six thousand years we've been in search
 Of what, but few could find;
('Tho', lighted by the gospel torch,)
 Sweet peace unto the mind.

Experience doth corroborate,
   The fact none can deny;
That Adam lost his first estate,
   And we have gone awry.
Thus, poor indeed we all may say,
   Without one bite to eat:
Likewise in debt, with nought to pay,
   And nak'd from head to feet!
Nothing on earth can satisfy,
   Our grand immortal part:
But extra light, from God on high,
   With purity of heart.
Obtain'd by faith in Christ, the Lord:
   Of all, in heaven and earth!
In whom, whate'er we need, is stor'd:
   Immensity of worth!
Rejoice, the feast is now prepar'd,
   Within the golden bowl:
And no expense or trouble spar'd,
   To satisfy the soul!
A vacuum, there ever was
   In man, till Christ was given,
Who purchas'd all, through whom he has,
   The privilege of heaven!
On earth, to be receiv'd in part,
   A satisfact'ry portion:
All true believers in the heart,
   Dwell, in the land of Goshen,
Where milk and honey ever flow,
   And fruits of Paradise;
In endless plenty to bestow,
   On all the good and wise.

By Him, whose bounty, love, and power ;
    Sheer wisdom, truth, and grace :
Keep pace, with every passing hour,
    In every time, and place.
Thus, what was lost; in Him is found,
    A never ending store :
Oceans of bliss, that have no bound ;
    Increasing evermore !
But what is in reserve for man,
    I'll not presume to state ;
For Jesus has the key, and plan,
    Which opens heaven's gate.
Whereby, who enter there behold,
    What eye hath never seen !
The bliss eternal can't be told,
    Till we with Him shall reign !

AN APOLOGY.

You may think I am harping, to sound my own
    praise,
    But hark you ! I don't care a straw ;
So long as I follow the Ancient of Days,
    If the worst, with the best you should know.
My losses, and crosses, afflictions, and grief,
    I cannot relate, till to-morrow ;
And as it won't come, to give present relief,
    I'll bury them all, without sorrow.

    2 w

Nor will I go seek them, to pester me more,
  Or harp on the discordant string ;
I've had quite enough of the gew-gaw before,
  Which never could harmony ring.
And this is the reason, I keep the world blind,
  To all my calamities here ;
Quite plenty you have, of your own, you will find,
  But, let them pass off in the rear.
You can not see a word, in the whole I have wrote,
  To distress, and torment you alive ;
Your welfare and mine, all my lifetime I've sought,
  United in which, we shall thrive.
To deprecate this, and the other bad thing,
  As we may imagine they are ;
Deprives us of all the sweet comfort they bring,
  And the laurels of christian war !
Our losses, and crosses, are oft in disguise,
  The greatest of blessings in time ;
Whereby, we shall win, the most elegant prize :
  And live, in a heavenly clime !
God forbid I should boast, except in the cross,
  My Saviour hath bid me take up :
In the ordeal of which, I part with the dross.
  And joyfully drink of the cup !

INDEX.

W. F. Pratt, Printer, Market Place, Stokesley.

A NEW AND ORIGINAL WORK,

ON THE OLDEST SUBJECT IN THE WORLD.

———

I AM requested by my youngest daughter, Elizabeth Wright, to announce her first appearance in the Literary World, as an Authoress; by whom may be expected, shortly, a Work of deep study, and research, designated

SINGULAR BIBLICAL NOTIFICATION

OF OCCURENCES IN ALL AGES OF THE WORLD,

OF THE NUMBERS THREE AND SEVEN;

Which first attracted her attention at the age of nine years, and commenced to write, solely for her own mental improvement, at the age of fifteen: since which time seven years have elapsed, and now the wonderful work seems nigh completion. Though herself reluctant to Publish, yet her friends (and friends to the religious public likewise,) have induced her to prepare it for the press, as something that may conduce to magnify the wisdom, and the order too, of Him, who first ordained the number three, (himself the Three in One,) a perfect number: likewise the number Seven, ever to be kept by man in holy reverence of Him who venerated this Himself; and bid us all, " Remember the Seventh (or Sabbath) Day, to keep it holy." Mark, in the numbers three and seven, all things were made complete, and ever shall remain, world without end.

www.ingramcontent.com/pod-product-compliance
Lightning Source LLC
Chambersburg PA
CBHW020557030726
47497CB00007B/1983